THE
Treasure
Hunt

REBECCA MARTIN

HARVEST HOUSE PUBLISHERS
EUGENE, OREGON

Cover by DesignByJulia, Woodland Park, Colorado

All Scripture quotations are from the King James Version of the Bible.

THE TREASURE HUNT

Copyright © 2013 Ridgeway Publishing
Illustrations © 2013 by Laura Yoder
Published by Harvest House Publishers
Eugene, Oregon 97402
www.harvesthousepublishers.com

Library of Congress Cataloging-in-Publication Data
    Martin, Rebecca.
    The treasure hunt / Rebecca Martin.
    pages cm. — (The Amish frontier series)
    Summary: In the early 1900s, after his family joins other Amish families on the Colorado frontier, young Joe, dreaming of an easier life, tries his hand at gold panning and learns some of life's truly golden lessons from an old prospector.
    ISBN 978-0-7369-6369-5 (pbk.)
    ISBN 978-0-7369-6370-1 (eBook)
    1. Amish—Colorado—Juvenile fiction. [1. Amish—Fiction. 2. Christian life—Fiction. 3. Frontier life—Colorado—Fiction. 4. Gold mines and mining—Fiction. 5. Colorado—History—1876-1950—Fiction.] I. Title.
    PZ7.M3641838Tr 2015
    [Fic]—dc23
                                                                              2014046243

Printed in the United States of America

        15 16 17 18 19 20 21 22 23 / BP-JH / 10 9 8 7 6 5 4 3 2 1

A Word from the Author

Although the characters are imaginary, this story is based on actual happenings. A number of the Amish families who moved to North Dakota in 1894 really did move again. In 1910 they moved to Colorado. The drought, fire, hailstorm, Mother's earache, Father's injured hand, Ben's journey to Ordway to find work, and his wife's trip to follow him actually happened as well. The gold rush, of course, is a historical fact, and Pikes Peak, that lofty mountain, is there for all to see.

1

Threshing Day

Three o'clock in the morning was certainly a strange time to be awake. In all her ten years of life, Lydia Yoder couldn't recall ever being awake at that time, but she couldn't help it because everybody else in the house was up too!

Nineteen-year-old Jake had started it. Lydia heard him scurrying past her bedroom door to the window at the end of the hall. Soon she heard more hurried footsteps as twelve-year-old Joe followed his brother to the window.

Before Lydia managed to get up, she heard the strange noises that had awakened her brothers. *Clang! Boom!* They were coming from the barnyard. *That must be the metal door of the steam tractor opening and closing as Hal adds more wood to the fire,* Lydia thought.

Seventeen-year-old Lisbet poked Lydia in the ribs. "Let's go to the window and watch!" The girls pattered across the chilly wooden floor and stared out toward the barn. There in the moonlight stood the steam tractor looking like a fire-breathing monster as clouds of smoke billowed from its stack. Every now and then, its "mouth" opened, and they could see orange flames as Hal, the fireman, fed it more wood.

"Poor fireman," whispered Lisbet. "He has to be up so early to make sure there's lots of steam when they want to start threshing. I wonder what time it is, anyway."

Just then they heard the deep-throated chiming of the clock in the kitchen below them. *Bong...bong...bong.* "Three o'clock!" Lydia whispered. She needn't have bothered to be quiet, though, because everyone seemed to be awake. Sounds were coming from the bedroom next door. Apparently even twenty-three-year-old Polly was excited enough about the threshing rig to leave her bed and watch the fireman.

Lisbet said knowingly, "Polly likes threshing time."

"You mean because Sam Peachy comes west to help with the threshing?" Lydia asked.

"Naturally."

Sam and Polly had become friends last year at threshing time. During the winter and most of the summer, Sam lived back East in Indiana, but come September he, along with dozens of other young men from the East, arrived to help with the threshing in North Dakota.

"I wonder when Polly and Sam will get married,"

said Lisbet. "Wouldn't that be exciting to have another wedding?"

Lydia nodded. Ben, their oldest brother, got married four years ago, and Lydia could still remember the wedding day, even though she'd been only six years old. Weddings were big events!

"We should get back to bed and sleep some more," said Lisbet with a shiver. "We have to rise early, you know."

"But not this early." Lydia giggled as she climbed back under the warm blanket.

"Probably at five thirty or whenever the whistle blows," Lisbet replied sleepily.

With so much excitement going on, Lydia found it hard to get back to sleep. Last night at dusk, Mr. Tim Forbes had come chugging in on the steam tractor, sitting high up on the seat like a king on his throne. Behind the tractor rumbled the mammoth separator, its long pipes swaying like a dragon's tail. What deep ruts the great steel lugs of the tractor's wheels made as it maneuvered into position! Precisely between two high stacks of sheaves, the separator was parked and ready to start threshing at the break of dawn.

Suddenly the sound of the steam whistle ripped through the darkness like an unearthly scream. Lydia flipped back the blanket and hopped out of bed in one motion. *I wonder if I slept since three o'clock. Maybe. It does seem like a long time ago since I stood shivering at the window to watch the fireman stoke the engine.*

Rustling into her dress and dashing down the stairs, Lydia managed to beat all her brothers and sisters to the kitchen. By the smells wafting from the big cookstove, Lydia guessed that Mother had been up for quite a while already. Bacon sizzled, coffee bubbled, and the eggs and potatoes were frying in the pan.

"How many plates do we need this morning?" Lydia asked Mother on her way to the pine cabinet Father had made to hold the china.

"Well, there's us. That's seven. And I think another seven men slept in the barn."

In the flickering light from the kerosene lamp, Lydia counted out fourteen plates. Carefully she arranged them around the long pine table that Father had also made. Lydia thought it was a very nice table, but Polly always said it wasn't as nice as the table they'd left behind in Indiana when they moved to North Dakota fifteen years ago. "That table," Polly would say, "was as smooth as a mirror."

Polly, Lisbet, and Lydia all helped Mother carry the food to the table. Outside on the porch they could hear the men washing up for breakfast. Lydia hung back shyly as the strangers came in and took their places at the table. Mr. Forbes, Hal the fireman, and the five young Amish men from Indiana sat down. None of them was Sam Peachy. Lydia knew that because she remembered that Sam had red hair like the color of a glowing chestnut, which was very different from Polly's red hair.

Steam rose from the plates of food and nearly hid the shadowy faces arranged around the table. It seemed strange to be eating breakfast so early that a lamp was needed. Usually one of the girls would milk the cow and the boys would feed the cattle before breakfast, but not today. The moment the sun came up, the threshers wanted to be done eating and ready to work.

Hal couldn't stay at the table very long. He wolfed down his food and then dashed out again to tend the fire. Nobody took time to talk. Lydia could almost feel the tension in the air. The men were like coiled springs ready to leap into action.

After breakfast Lydia simply could not stay inside to wash dishes. The sun was coming up, and she wanted to be outside watching the excitement! Mother let her go, providing she would help with the housework later on.

More young men arrived from the neighboring farms where they had spent the night, and soon everyone was in position and ready to start.

"Awww-RIGHT!" yelled Mr. Forbes. That was the signal to begin. The great long belt from the engine to the separator began to turn slowly and then faster and faster. The steam engine puffed harder. The white canvas of the carriers revolved, gathering speed until the separator's *chug-chug* settled into a steady roar.

From high up on the stacks, men threw sheaves of wheat down onto the platform. Here the band cutters worked frantically to remove the twine from the sheaves and pass them on to the feeders. How fast the feeders worked! Their arms flashed back and forth as their forks fed a steady stream of grain onto the carriers. Finally the fearful looking teeth of the separator gobbled up the sheaves.

Lydia watched the men feed the hungry machine.

Soon the yellow straw blew from the pipes at the back. Some men stayed busy stacking the straw. When the stack was big enough, it was dragged away by a large rake-like apparatus, which was pulled by horses. At the side of the machine, still more men flew into action, bagging the stream of golden grain into the white cotton sacks Father had brought from the elevator. Two men were kept busy carrying the filled bags into the granary of the barn, where they would be stored until Father had time to haul them to the elevator.

At midmorning neighbors began arriving with their teams and wagons. Those two tall stacks of sheaves would soon be whittled down to nothing. As far as the eye could see, out in the fields stood thousands of stocks waiting to be brought in and threshed. How swiftly the men worked at piling the wagons high with sheaves! One after the other, the loaded wagons rolled in from the fields. The threshing machine must not be allowed a single idle minute, except at dinnertime when the men stopped to eat.

Mother and the girls had lots of work to do to prepare dinner. Lydia peeled potatoes until she thought her fingers would drop off. Great pots of potatoes, turnips, and other vegetables were set to boil on top of the stove. They had boiled the ham yesterday, and now they sliced it into thick slabs and piled it onto platters. For dessert they dished up bowls and bowls of stewed dried fruit. In the oven were pans of sweet rice pudding chock full of raisins—a special treat to be served with thick clotted cream from the cool cellar.

At noon Hal blew the whistle. "Is everything ready?" Polly asked nervously, scurrying back and forth from the stove to the long plank tables in the yard. Basins of water stood on the lawn for the men to use to wash up. They threw their hats in a heap and began splashing their faces with the cool water. Most of them were black with dust!

When everyone was seated, silence descended on the group. They bowed their heads to ask the blessing. How quiet it seemed after all the noise of the forenoon! Then spoons clattered on the plates, and the food began to disappear. The women kept busy refilling platters and bowls.

"Will there be any rice pudding left for us?" Lydia whispered to Lisbet as she watched the threshers heap their plates.

"Oh, surely a little bit," Lisbet assured her, "but I'd forgotten how much threshers can eat."

"The men work hard," Polly reminded her sisters.

And so did the women. No sooner had they finished clearing away the noon meal than it was time to start preparing supper!

2

Pikes Peak Stories

After two days it was over. All of Father's many acres of wheat had been threshed, and Mr. Forbes moved on with his big steam tractor and separator—on to the next farm and the next and the next. North Dakota in 1909 was full of wheat farms.

Of course the workers from back East did not go home as soon as the Yoders' wheat was done. They stayed to help on all the other farms as well. Sam Peachy would be in the area for at least two months.

He came to the Yoders' house for supper that first Saturday evening. Lydia was so fascinated by his gleaming mop of chestnut hair that she almost forgot to eat. Lydia wished she had hair like that—or like Jake's or Polly's. It was funny, though, because Polly wished she had straw-blond hair like Lydia's.

Sam Peachy was a restless, talkative young man. He asked lots of questions and told lots of stories. On this Saturday evening, he was full of stories about a trip he had recently taken. "Before I came up here this summer, I traveled to Pikes Peak Country," he began as soon as his bowl was filled with soup.

"Pikes Peak Country? Where's that?" Jake asked.

Sam grinned at him. "Ever heard of Colorado?"

Before Jake could reply, Joe piped up. "That's where they had a gold rush. We learned about it at school. Somebody found gold in a stream, and thousands of people rushed to Colorado to get rich."

Father gave him an amused smile. "When was that?" The whole family knew how much Joe liked history. People kept telling him that he should teach school someday. He was so good at storing knowledge in his head.

"The gold rush started in the 1850s," Joe replied promptly.

"And did the gold seekers all get rich?" Father asked.

Joe shrugged. "Some did, but when the gold ran out, they left. Then not too long ago in 1892, I think, there was another gold strike in Colorado."

As if he had heard enough stories about the gold rush, Sam said, "The Amish who are interested in Colorado are thinking of a different kind of gold—wheat. You can buy land there for about eighteen dollars an acre. With prices like that, it should be possible to make money at wheat farming."

Father's eyebrows rose. "Do you mean to say there are Amish people buying land in Colorado?"

"Yes. Don't you get the *Sugarcreek Budget*?" Sam asked. "You don't? Well, you could read about it in there. In August a land agency placed a big ad telling about the new Amish settlement in eastern Colorado. You can get a free train ticket to go see the area—providing you buy land." Sam's green eyes glowed as he talked.

Lydia glanced at Polly. The expression on her face was hard to figure out. *Is she excited about Colorado too? If she marries Sam, and if he moves to Colorado...* Suddenly a burning question filled Lydia's mind. She didn't often speak when visitors were present, but she simply couldn't wait. She had to know. She blurted out, "How far away is Colorado?"

Everyone looked at Lydia as if surprised that a little girl had spoken up. Lydia felt her face grow hot and wished she could disappear under the table.

"Colorado," Sam answered slowly, "is about two days and two nights by train from here. I know because I came directly from there to here."

"So it must be three or four hundred miles," Father said after briefly calculating the distance. "That's about the same as from here to Indiana."

Lydia let out a small sigh, small enough so nobody would hear. *Three hundred miles! That sounds like a long,*

long way. Is Polly going to live three hundred miles from home when she gets married?

Sam, of course, had no idea what Lydia was thinking. He was saying, "And remember, your train ticket is free. I've paid for mine, but if I buy land, I'll get the money refunded."

Jake sat up straight, his eyes shining. "Are you going to buy land?"

But before Sam could answer, Joe asked just as eagerly, "Is it near the place where they found gold?"

Chuckling, Father held up his hands. "Whoa there. Hold your horses."

Sam laughed too. "Have you heard the name of the town where the Amish are buying? It's Wild Horse."

Now everyone had to laugh, including Polly. Father had more questions about Colorado and asked, "Has this land ever been tilled?"

Sam shook his head. "It's virgin prairie. Tall grass as far as the eye can see."

"That sounds just like North Dakota when we came here," Father commented with a glance at Mother.

"So the settlers in Colorado can build sod houses," Mother said. "Sod houses are nice. They're cool in summer."

Lydia knew what a sod house was like. The Kanagys still had one that they used for storage, and Polly often told stories about the early days in North Dakota when nearly everyone lived in houses made of sod.

Sam cleaned up the last bit of his apple pie. "If I bought land in Colorado, I would go down there and build me a wooden house. No need to live like savages."

"What do the Amish intend to plant?" Father asked.

Sam pushed back his chair. "Mostly wheat, I think. The topsoil is deep—three or four feet—and it's sandy."

"Hmmm, sounds like sugar beet country. Sugar beets thrive in sandy soil."

"Then Ben should move to Colorado!" said Joe. "He's always trying to raise sugar beets, but every fall the frost comes too early. In Colorado he'd have a longer growing season."

"And he could afford to buy land too," Jake said. "Eighteen dollars an acre doesn't sound like much. Up here land is sky-high at eighty dollars an acre."

Ben and his wife and children lived in a small house on the corner of the Yoder property. Lydia knew that Ben wanted to buy a farm of his own, but he couldn't afford it. And besides, there were no farms for sale nearby.

Joe turned to Father and said, "We should tell Ben about Colorado, shouldn't we?"

Father gave him a slow, wise smile. "Let's not get too excited, son."

It was Mother who finally asked, "Why do you call this area Pikes Peak Country?"

Sam's eyes gleamed some more. "Where the Amish are

buying is less than a hundred miles from the Rocky Mountains. There's one especially high peak called Pikes Peak. It's over fourteen thousand feet high, and you can see it clearly from sixty miles away! I saw this little rhyme in the *Sugarcreek Budget*:

> Now if a home you wish to seek,
> Come where you can view old Pikes Peak.
> The land where plains and mountains meet,
> And our farmers grow macaroni wheat.

Lydia was glad when the meal was over. All this talk about strange, faraway lands gave her an uneasy feeling. She did not like to think of people moving hundreds of miles away.

Soon it was Sunday, the best day of the week. The Yoder family walked a mile and a half down the road to church, which was being held at John Swartzentruber's home. As far back as Lydia could remember, there had been two church districts, the north district and the south district with ministers for each one. But Polly still remembered the days when there were no ministers at all here in North Dakota and the only time they had church was when a visiting minister came from the East.

As the Yoder family neared the Swartzentruber farm, Lydia quickened her steps. There in front of the house were Mary and Susanna Swartzentruber, welcoming everyone with big smiles.

What would I ever do without Mary and Susanna? Lydia asked herself as she ran to greet them. *It would be terrible to move away from such good friends.*

Imagine Lydia's surprise when even the minister, in his sermon that morning, spoke of a little girl who moved far away from home! Preacher Josiah told the story of the little slave girl who helped save the great Captain Naaman's life. "There are not many stories in the Bible that tell about a little girl," said Josiah, "but in this story, we read about a 'little maid.' Can you imagine how terrible it must have been for this little Hebrew maid when the Syrian soldiers broke into her home in Israel and carried her away as a captive to a strange land?

"But this little maid did not lose her faith in God. Oh no. There was no doubt in her mind that God could heal Naaman's leprosy through His prophet Elisha. You see, this little maid was the slave of Naaman's wife, and that is why she knew about the great captain's illness. So one day she summoned her courage and told her mistress about the prophet."

Josiah went on to tell the rest of the story about how the prophet commanded Naaman to wash in the Jordan River and how the captain felt it was beneath his dignity to do so.

But Lydia's mind stayed with that little maid of Israel who was torn from her parents and made a slave in a strange land. How wonderful that because of this little girl's faith a great captain was healed of leprosy!

3

More Colorado Talk

Monday was wash day. Lydia, Lisbet, and Polly all took turns at the washing machine. First the clothes were swished around and around in the sudsy water while they jiggled the tub back and forth. Then they had to crank all the clothing through the wringer. The part Lydia enjoyed the best was hanging the clean clothes on the line in the yard.

This morning there was a strong wind from the west. How it tore at the dresses and aprons and trousers as Lydia pinned them up! "The wash will dry nicely today," remarked Mother as she passed by on her way to the garden.

When the wash basket was empty, Lydia found Mother down on her knees, digging carrots. "Will we have carrots for dinner?" Lydia asked.

"Yes, we will. Aren't the carrots nice this year?" said Mother, holding up a big orange carrot.

"Mmmm. May I have one?" With her apron, Lydia wiped the soil from the carrot. It crunched crisply between her teeth. "Mother, do you really think Sam Peachy will buy land in Colorado?"

Lydia fretfully wondered if Polly was going to move to Colorado.

Mother sat back on her heels and looked up. With one hand she smoothed back the ringlets of gray hair that had escaped from her covering. "I don't know, Lydia. Maybe he will."

"Would that mean Polly is going to move to Colorado?" There, the question was out—the painful question that had been bothering her since Saturday evening.

Mother bent to dig more carrots. "Yes, it probably would." Mother's voice sounded strange, as if there was a lump in her throat. Something told Lydia that if Polly moved away, it would be just as hard on Mother as it would be for her.

"Why can't Sam just get a home here in North Dakota?"

"You heard what the men said," Mother replied, still in that muffled voice. "It's very hard to buy land here."

"Well, yes, I know that."

"Sam is not the only one who'd be interested in homesteading in Colorado. Ben and some others would be interested too. You see, young men who didn't homestead here in North Dakota could get land very cheaply in Colorado. Father and I homesteaded here, so we would need to pay more for land in Colorado. But it would still be much less than here."

Lydia moved closer to Mother. "You mean *we* are interested too?" The thought left her breathless.

Mother got to her feet while holding the pail of carrots. She patted Lydia's shoulder. "I don't know if 'interested' is the right word, but I can tell you this much. We're praying about it."

"Why would we want to move?" Lydia asked, keeping step with Mother as she hurried to the house.

"For one thing, the wheat price is very low, Lydia. Father says there will be very little money left over by the time he has paid for the threshing, the twine, and the bags. We might not even earn enough money to buy seeds next spring. So that is one reason why we would consider making a new start somewhere else. And another reason… Well, Lydia, if our children are talking of moving so far away—"

"Then you want to go too," Lydia finished for her.

As she went back to jiggling the wash tub, her feelings were as mixed-up as the clothing that splashed about in the suds. Colorado sounded exciting—but frightening too.

That night before they slept, Lydia told Lisbet about the conversation with Mother in the garden. Lisbet sucked in her breath. "That sounds as if Father and Mother are actually thinking of moving to Colorado."

"Are you glad?" Lydia asked.

For a minute there was only the sound of Lisbet's breathing in the darkness. Then she said, "I don't want to move. I like it here. Our friends are here."

"That's just how I feel, but I didn't tell Mother that."

"What I can't understand—" Lisbet said slowly. "I mean, Father often talks of how God blesses us with happy hearts, even if we don't have all the things we'd like to have. Why isn't he content here? Why would he dream of making more money in Colorado if he keeps saying it's not money that makes us happy, but trusting and obeying God?"

"You should ask Mother those questions. I wondered about that too, but I didn't know how to put it into words. Ask her tomorrow."

"Well, I'll see…" Lisbet's voice had grown sleepy. Soon the two sisters drifted off to sleep.

That night it rained, and the next day the air had a sharp, cold tang to it. "We'll have frost soon," Mother said, giving voice to her prediction. "We'd better bring in the last of the pumpkins, beans, and corn."

All day Mother and the girls trundled back and forth between the garden and the cellar, bringing in the late vegetables for winter storage. Joe, Ben, and Jake went to help thresh at another farm with the Yoders' one team of horses while Father took the other team to haul his first load of wheat to the elevator.

Toward evening Lisbet saw Father far in the distance across the prairie coming back home. "I hope the wheat price is better now," she said wistfully as she loaded a pumpkin onto the little wagon.

Mother added another one to the load. "What makes you say that?" she asked curiously.

"Because…" Lisbet said and then hesitated. "Because if we could make more money here, we wouldn't have to move to Colorado."

Mother stood with both hands on top of the pumpkin, looking at the seventeen-year-old. "We have no plans to move away."

"No, but you're thinking about it."

"Praying about it. We want to do God's will," said Mother firmly.

"But, Mother, why would we want to move? I thought we're supposed to be content and not always wishing to have more. I thought we're to be happy even if we don't have all the things we'd like." Lisbet's words came out in a rush.

"Very true," Mother said quietly. "We are not discontented. We are just concerned about our children's future. If they want to marry and raise families, they need homes of their own."

"I wish Sam Peachy weren't putting these ideas about Colorado into people's heads," Lisbet mumbled. She glanced toward Polly, who was out of hearing distance.

Mother gave a little sigh. "Lisbet, try to believe that we are truly seeking God's will."

"Okay," Lisbet answered sincerely.

"Let's go and help unhitch the wagon," Lydia suggested when she saw that Father's team had driven up to the barn. She and Lisbet ran across the yard to the team of black horses. In spite of the raw wind, Ned and King were streaked with sweat.

Speaking to Father across King's broad back, Lisbet asked hopefully, "How was the wheat price?"

"Lower than ever," Father answered, managing to sound cheerful, "and Trevor, at the elevator, says the price is bound to go lower still when all the wheat starts pouring in from this area."

"It isn't fair," Lisbet said as she unhooked the trace.

"There's nothing we can do about it," Father replied matter-of-factly.

"But think of all the hard work you did, all those hours of plowing and planting and harvesting." Lisbet replied, sounding as if she was almost ready to cry.

Lydia glanced at her in alarm. Father said reassuringly, "At least we won't go hungry." And with that, he led the team to the barn.

4

Train Trip

As North Dakota's brief summer gave way to fall, every day held the same activities for the men. Every day Father hauled wheat to the elevator. Every day Ben, Jake, and Joe went threshing.

And every day it seemed as if the threshers talked about Colorado. In the evening at the supper table, Jake and Joe spoke of Pikes Peak, homesteading, and sugar-beet farming in Colorado. Polly always listened with interest, while Lisbet and Lydia wished their brothers would talk about something else.

As October drew to a close, so did the threshing season. Not long afterward, Father made a startling announcement. Father and seven other men were going to Colorado to look around. Ben was going, but his wife, Barbara, would stay at home. Jake was going too. "They are the ones who'd be getting land under the homestead law if we decide to settle there. Any land I'd buy would be higher priced because the government allows you only one free homestead."

Lydia and Lisbet had been doing the supper dishes when Father made his announcement. The two girls immediately stopped and turned to look at each other once the words were spoken. Lydia noticed that Lisbet appeared just as stunned as she was. They both realized that it really was happening!

Jake and Joe sat on the bench near the stove, grinning at each other. Obviously this was no surprise to them. "I just wish I could go too," Joe said wistfully.

"Maybe later," Father said with a smile.

Lydia wanted to cry out, "Stop! Not so fast," but she knew that would be no use, and so she asked in a tremulous voice, "When are you leaving?"

"On Thursday. I'll buy the tickets tomorrow," Father replied. "We'll be gone for more than a week." He looked at Joe. "You'll have to be the man of the house for Mother and for Barbara too."

But that was not the way it turned out. On Thursday morning Jake was sick. He had a sore throat and high fever, and his ears ached. Poor Jake simply wasn't able to go on the trip! Much to Joe's delight, he was allowed to go instead.

As he boarded the train with Father, Joe was so excited

that he thought he would burst. Only once before had he been on a train. As a small boy, he'd gone along to visit Grandpa and Grandma in Indiana.

They traveled south, down through the plains of North Dakota, and before they knew it, they were in South Dakota. "It doesn't look any different from North Dakota," Joe remarked to Sam Peachy, with whom he shared a seat.

"Not now, but wait until we get to the badlands," Sam told him with a mysterious smile.

"What are the badlands?"

"Oh, it's a place where all the bad people live," Sam replied airily. When Joe looked worried, Sam chuckled and said, "That was just a joke. It's the land that's 'bad.' You'll see. I'm told that when the Sioux Indians were at war with the United States, the badlands provided good hiding places for the Indians."

The railroad rambled south between rolling hills and followed the James River for many miles. Just as Joe began to wonder when they would ever turn west, they changed trains, crossed the Missouri River, and did just that. Now the land began to change. Rugged ridges and steep valleys carved their way through the plains.

"Look at that strangely shaped hill!" exclaimed Joe, pointing at a hill that rose steeply on all sides and then ended in a flat top.

"You'll see lots more hills like that," Sam told him. "They're called buttes."

Sure enough, another steep, flat-topped hill came into view. Then several more appeared. "Say, are these the badlands you talked about?" Joe asked.

Sam laughed. "Oh no, the badlands are much worse than this."

To Joe the train seemed to be traveling uphill much of the time. Peering westward he asked Sam, "That dark ridge along the horizon, is that a mountain ridge? Are those the Rocky Mountains?"

"Not yet. What you see are the Black Hills. The Sioux Indians called them that because they look black from here. They're all covered with pine trees, you see. That means they're not nearly as high as the Rockies."

"And those are still not the badlands?"

Sam shook his head. "We'll change trains in Rapid City and head south again. Then we'll see the badlands. You'll know them when you see them. Nothing grows there."

Sam was right. The badlands were unmistakable. What a scene of desolation! What strangely shaped cliffs. The steep gullies were carved into the limestone! Joe had never seen anything like it. "It makes me feel like I'm on the moon or something," he said to Sam.

"Almost gives you the creeps, doesn't it?" Sam replied cheerfully.

"You sure couldn't make a living in this area—not from farming, anyway."

Soon after leaving the badlands, they crossed the border into Nebraska, which held few surprises. The whole state was made up of plains, hills, and valleys, broken only by occasional streams and rivers, the largest one being the North Platte River.

The boys enjoyed looking out the train window.

The conductor on this train took a liking to Joe and Sam and came back repeatedly to talk with them. "That river's the South Platte now," he said, pointing out the window. "And that means we'll soon cross the border into Colorado. Yep, here we are now in Colorado."

"Will we see the Rockies soon?" asked Joe.

"Oh, it'll be a while, but it's a nice, clear day, so keep watching toward the west. The mountains will look like a jagged purple blur along the horizon."

That was exactly what Joe saw later on when the sun was going down, a jagged purple blur. "Are those mountains or just clouds?"

The conductor stooped to peer out the window. "That's the Rockies all right. Good for you! You saw them first."

That night they came to the bustling town of Denver. In the morning the mountains were much closer. "Looks like I could just walk over and touch them," Joe said to Father, who smiled and said the mountains were farther away than they appeared.

The sheer, rocky peaks took Joe's breath away. He couldn't tear his eyes away from them. He felt sorry for Ben, who sat on the other side of the train and, therefore, had no west-facing window.

After leaving Denver they traveled east again on the Union Pacific Railroad. Joe was sorry to be traveling away from the mountains, but then Sam told him, "Now we watch for Pikes Peak."

Nobody had to tell Joe what it was he was looking at when the peak came into view. He knew the kingly mountain rising head and shoulders above the more distant mountains had to be it. He knew it before Sam cried, "There she is! There's Pikes Peak!"

It was beautiful. Its high, snowcapped ramparts gleamed in the sunlight. Joe thought, *It sure would be something to live where I could see this mountain every day!*

At a town named Limon, Sam announced, "Some Amish are buying in this area. Elbert County, I think it's called, but we're going on to Cheyenne County."

Wild Horse. The name on the weather-beaten sign seemed to jump out at Joe. He turned excitedly to Sam and asked, "Is this the place?"

"Sure is," Sam replied with a grin. "I told you. Wild Horse, Cheyenne County, Colorado."

They quickly gathered their baggage and got ready to disembark. The land agent was right there at the station with his Ford car to take them out to the homesteads. As they drove, Joe turned his head this way and that, trying to take in all the scenery. It was just as Sam had said—tall, waving grass as far as the eye could see. "Does this look like North Dakota did when you first got there?" he asked Father.

Father's eyes had a faraway look. "Yes, it does."

The land agent kept up a steady chatter. He told them about the land, where to buy lumber, seeds, and other things like that. When they finally stepped out of the car, they found themselves standing near a creek that reminded Joe of the creek back home.

While the men began shoveling the soil to see what it was like, Joe went to explore the creek. He wondered if anybody had ever panned for gold along this creek. *Maybe there are pebbles of gold lying down there beneath the rippling water!*

Joe heard a sudden noise, like a twig cracking on the bank above him. He quickly turned to look up and caught a fleeting glimpse of a moving brown object. *Was that a rabbit? Or was it a man's boot disappearing into the underbrush?* Joe wasn't sure.

Months later he was to recall this moment in vivid detail.

5

Moving

B ut, Mother, what if Jake and Sam haven't got our house ready for us when we get there?" Ever since leaving North Dakota, this worry had gnawed at Lydia's mind and caused her to fret.

"Oh, the house will be far enough along that we can move into it," Mother said soothingly. "After all, they started building two months ago."

From the seat behind Mother and Lydia, Polly spoke up. "We'll survive, Lydia. Why, when we arrived in North Dakota in 1894, there were no houses at all! Just prairie! We all had to get to work to build that sod house."

"You're always talking about that," Lydia grumbled, "but we're not going to make sod houses. Real, wooden houses take longer to build."

"Sod houses are real too," Polly insisted. "I wouldn't mind living in one again."

"Hmmm," sniffed Lydia. With that, the girls fell silent, each staring out the train window at the jagged skyline of the Rocky Mountains in the distance. Lydia still felt she needed to pinch herself to make sure this was real. It was January 1910, and the Yoder family was moving—actually *moving* to Colorado! They had been on the train for several days now. They had seen South Dakota with its Black Hills and badlands. They had trundled through Nebraska and crossed the North Platte and South Platte rivers. They were now in Colorado, and soon, according to Joe, who enjoyed pointing out the sights from his seat behind Polly and Lisbet, they would see Pikes Peak. It was all very exciting.

Still, that worry about the house gnawed at Lydia. How sorry she had been to leave their snug home in North Dakota. *Yes, Sam and Jake had promised they would have a house ready when we arrive, but would they really? What if something has gone wrong? There are so many unknowns when moving to a strange, faraway land!*

Mother seemed to sense how Lydia felt. "Remember the story of the little maid of Israel," she said softly. "Syrian soldiers broke into her home and stole her from her parents and then carried her hundreds of miles away to be a slave in Naaman's house. God was with that little girl. He is with us today."

Lydia gave Mother a grateful smile. She felt better already.

Suddenly Joe shouted, "That's Pikes Peak!"

Before Lydia's eyes, the great white peak seemed to rise slowly from the horizon. Mother murmured some verses from Psalms, "I will lift up mine eyes unto the hills, from whence cometh my help. My help cometh from the LORD, which made heaven and earth."

◇◇◇◇◇

It was evening when the train slowed down and stopped in Wild Horse. "This used to be a busy town," Joe informed them. "It was built in the days of the gold rush, you see, but it's become a sort of ghost town now."

"Why a ghost town?" Lydia giggled nervously. She didn't believe in ghosts, of course, but still—

Joe said, "A ghost town is what they call a place where there are a lot of unoccupied buildings. See those boarded up windows? They're that way because those stores are not in use anymore."

"Oh, I see," said Lydia, feeling relieved. "What do we do now? Do we get off the train?"

"You may if you like," replied Father from his seat beside Joe, "but this train car is being left here for the homesteaders. Not everyone was able to send carpenters ahead to build houses the way we did."

"Will Jake be here to fetch us tonight?" asked Joe.

Father shook his head. "We didn't let him know exactly when we'd be coming, just that it would be in January. We'll sleep on the train car again tonight. Tomorrow we'll get our team out of the livestock car and drive out to our home."

"Jake's home, you mean," Joe said with a grin. The place was in Jake's name because he could still get cheap land under the homesteading law. Father was buying a section right next to Jake's homestead, but the house was being built on Jake's land. The law said that the homesteader had to live on his land to secure the title.

So Lydia spent one more night with Lisbet in the upper bunk of the train car.

In the morning the light coming in the window had a blinding white quality. "Why, there's snow on the ground!" Lydia exclaimed when she looked out. "So it does snow in Colorado!"

"Of course it does," answered Lisbet. "We haven't moved to Florida or anything."

After boiling some eggs for breakfast on the train car's stove, the Yoders set out across the prairie with Ned and King. They piled the wagon as high as they dared with household goods. The girls squeezed in among the baggage, but Joe decided he would rather walk. At first it was a challenge to keep up with the team, frisky as they were after days on the train, but after a while the horses settled down, and Joe could keep pace.

Finally they saw a partially finished house in the distance. Several men were climbing about on the roof. "That can't be ours," Lydia said. "They are only putting the shingles on the roof, and there are no walls yet."

Lydia saw the unfinished house and wondered what would come next.

Father turned and said slowly, "But that is our place, Lydia. It seems they didn't make as much progress on the house as they'd hoped."

Lydia groaned. "What are we going to do?"

"It's okay," Mother said, assuring her. "Remember that the train car is available for a few more nights if we need it."

"Once we're helping with the house, it'll be finished in a hurry," Father declared optimistically. "Who knows? We might even get the siding on today."

As the family talked, they noticed that one of the men had scrambled down from the roof and was running to meet them. It was Jake, looking worried and unhappy. "Didn't you get my letter?" It was the first thing he said to his family.

"No, we didn't," Father answered in surprise.

"I wrote to tell you that we needed another two weeks to build the house. We had trouble getting the lumber, you see."

Father got down from the wagon and began unhitching. "Well, we're here to help now! Do you have the lumber for the siding?"

"Yes. It just came yesterday. It's in that pile over there." Jake indicated where the siding was stacked with a wave of his hand.

Father looked around at the girls and Joe. "How many helpers do I have for fastening siding to the walls?"

Lisbet hopped down from the wagon. Polly, Lydia and

Mother followed her lead. "We'll all help if we can. We have to do something to keep warm," Mother said cheerfully.

"As soon as we have one wall closed in, we'll set up our cookstove. We brought everything that's needed for a chimney, I think. Then we can warm up by the stove," Father said as he planned out their day.

And what a day it was! The girls discovered that they did have some carpenter skills. Everyone pitched in to raise the walls. Lydia didn't hammer any nails, but she helped carry the lumber and hold the clapboards in place while Father pounded nails.

At noon the men lugged the heavy cookstove from the wagon and set it up in the kitchen, which had only one wall as yet. Mother built a fire in the stove and warmed some soup, which they ate while huddled around the stove. The wind coming down from Pikes Peak was cold, as if chilled by that faraway, icy peak.

By nightfall most of the clapboards were in place, so the Yoders unloaded their belongings into the house and drove back to town. They were happy to reach the cozy warmth of the train car. As night closed in, the other six families from North Dakota also returned to the train car. Lydia's friends Veronica and Rebecca Miller said, "We're going to rent a house here in town until we can build one on our farm. There are plenty of empty houses here in town."

"What does your rented house look like?" Lydia questioned, settling into a seat with the other two girls.

"Oh, it's old and dusty and cobwebby, and the windows are all boarded up," Rebecca reported cheerfully.

Veronica put in, "But we've cleaned most of it already, and it was nice and warm after we put up our stove."

"My brother Ben is going to rent a house too," Lydia told them. "I shouldn't have worried about a house for us since there are so many around that are not being used."

"Did you worry? I thought Jake came down here ahead of you to build a house," Veronica said in surprise.

Lydia smiled sheepishly. "Yes, I worried they wouldn't have it done. I guess I'm not a very good pioneer."

"Why, our parents went off to North Dakota and had nothing but sod houses," Rebecca said. "They were real pioneers!"

As soon as she could, Lydia wrote a letter to Mary and Susanna Swartzentruber, back in North Dakota.

Dear Mary and Susanna,

Our house is almost finished, and we are glad because the weather is cold. It is not as cold as North Dakota, though. Right now there is no snow on the ground, but it snowed the first night we were here.

The name of our nearest town is Wild Horse. I think that is a funny name for a town, don't you? Maybe someday I will find out why our town has that name.

The train ride was fun. I liked sleeping in the upper bunk. The swaying was like a ship on the ocean. I hope you get to take a ride on a train too one day.

Your friend,

Lydia

Not long afterward, a letter came from her friends. Mary and Susanna had big news for Lydia.

Dear Lydia,

Guess what! We are going to move too! I wish we would come to Colorado, but we are moving to Montana. The name of our nearest town will be Glendive. Do you know where Montana is? It is right beside North Dakota and up by the Canadian border. Montana is the third largest state of the USA. It is really big! There's lots of room in Montana for you too if you don't like it in Colorado...

Lydia stopped reading and stared thoughtfully out the window. She did not want to move away from Colorado because moving was hard work. But she did wish that Mary and Susanna Swartzentruber did not live so far away.

6

To the Hospital

With Colorado's dry, pleasant weather, the families were able to keep building all winter. The sun shone nearly every day, and the temperature frequently went up to forty degrees at noon.

The nights, of course, were colder. Chilly winds poked through the cracks of hastily built houses. One morning when Lydia came downstairs to the kitchen, Mother wasn't there. Polly told her gravely, "Mother has a bad earache, and Father went to get the doctor."

"Oh," said Lydia in alarm. "Is it really bad this time?" Mother had been plagued with earaches for years, especially during the frigid North Dakota winters.

Polly cracked an egg and let it drop into the sizzling pan. "It must be pretty bad if Father's getting the doctor."

"I had hoped Mother's earaches would be better here in Colorado since it's warmer," Lisbet said as she caught on to the conversation after coming in from the barn with the milk.

"So did I," Lydia echoed. She didn't like to think of Mother lying in the bedroom in pain. "What do you think the doctor will do to her?"

"I have no idea," Polly confessed. "There's a car coming up the road now. Maybe that's him."

Father returned home at the same time as the Ford chugged in the driveway. Dr. Crawford was a short dumpy man. He barely looked at the girls when he entered the house, but went straight to the bedroom with Father. Lydia heard low voices in there. Only a short time later, Dr. Crawford and Father came out of the bedroom and left the house. Out by the car, they talked for a few minutes, and then the doctor drove away.

Father hurried back inside. "Is breakfast getting cold?" he asked apologetically. "I need just a minute to talk with Mother again, and then I'll be out for breakfast." Once more he went into the bedroom.

By the time he reappeared, the boys had arrived for breakfast too. "Mother says she'll stay in bed," Father informed the family as they all took their places at the table.

Lydia stared at the egg on her plate. Somehow she didn't feel very hungry knowing Mother was in bed too sick to eat.

"Dr. Crawford says Mother needs to have an operation on her ear," Father told them. "If she doesn't, she might lose her hearing in that ear."

"Will she have to go to the hospital?" Polly asked in alarm.

"Yes. To Denver. Today, if possible," answered Father.

"How will she get there?" Jake asked.

"By train. Dr. Crawford has gone to see a few more patients up the road, and on the way back, he will pick up Mother and take her to the train station," Father explained.

"Won't you go along?" asked Lisbet.

Father looked troubled. "I would like to, of course, but Mother may need to be gone for a week." He cleared his throat. "Mother thinks I should stay here with you." He paused again. "I don't want to scare anyone, but Gregory Higgins told me yesterday that there's a big danger of prairie fires these days. The dead grass becomes very dry and brittle when there's no snow. All it takes is a spark from a passing train. There was a big fire north of here last week. So now you know why Mother wants me to stay. Dr. Crawford will stop at the Millers to see if Catherine can go with Mother to the hospital."

Catherine. That was Veronica's mother. Lydia's mind was whirling as she tried to take it all in. Mother was going to the hospital. Prairie fires. A multitude of questions tumbled through her mind. "But what should we do if there's a prairie fire?" she asked tremulously.

"I am planning to plow a firebreak today," Father told her kindly.

Polly spoke up. "I remember the prairie fire we had in North Dakota. The firebreak you plowed saved our house."

"But can you plow in winter?" Jake asked.

"That may be a problem," Father said, acknowledging his son's concern. "Even though it's not terribly cold, the ground is partly frozen. The other thing we can do—if there's a fire—is to burn toward it. We can start a fire of our own, you know, well away from the buildings, and burn off all the grass so the fire has nothing to feed on."

"If that's necessary, then I'm certainly glad that you will stay here," Jake said. "I wouldn't know how to control a fire that's meant to stop another fire."

"I hope it won't be needed," said Father. "Oh, here's the doctor back already. I'll go help Mother get ready."

Lydia slipped over to the window. "Catherine is in the doctor's car. She certainly got ready on short notice."

Soon Mother emerged from the bedroom wearing her bonnet and shawl. How pale and drawn her face looked! And her eyes were glazed with pain. "Well, girls, I know you'll be okay while I'm gone," she said, trying to smile. "This will be good practice for you, Polly, to keep house without me."

The wedding! In all the excitement, Lydia had forgotten about the wedding. Sam and Polly's wedding was to be in a month from now. "I hope you get better soon," Lydia called after Mother.

◇◇◇◇◇

The house was a desolate place without Mother. Lydia wandered around, not knowing what to do and wishing she could go to school. The land agent had promised that a school would be started in the neighborhood, but that was not to be until next fall. In the meantime Grandma Kanagy held some reading and arithmetic classes once a week for the children of the settlers.

"I wish we had a dog," Lydia complained. "Then I could at least go out and play with him. Joe's always busy these days, helping somewhere with the building. He never plays with me anymore."

Lisbet said irritably, "I wish you would stop your whining, Lydia! Think of Mother having to travel all that way with an earache. Compared to her, we have nothing to complain about."

"Why don't you go out and see how Father's getting along with his plowing?" Polly spoke up pleasantly. She was never idle these days. She was always sewing or making rugs or piecing quilts.

"Well, all right," Lydia said grumpily. She put on her coat and scarf and went outside. Tiny puffs of clouds were scattered across the blue sky, chased from horizon to horizon by a strong north wind. She could hear Father talking to the horses as she neared him. "Come on, Ned. Giddyap, King."

When Father saw Lydia, he stopped the horses and wiped his forehead. "Plowing is not going too well. The plowshare simply does not want to stay in the frozen ground."

Lydia stared at the pitiful strip of plowed ground. "Then I hope we don't have a fire."

"Well, I'll keep on trying to plow."

"Would the creek help stop a fire?"

"Yes, but it doesn't flow between us and the railroad, which is where the fire would come from." Father peered toward the north. The railroad was far enough away that they couldn't see the train, but they often heard the whistle. On days like today, when the wind was from the north, the rumbling and the whistle were loud and clear.

Father clucked to the horses, and they went on plowing. Lydia wandered over to the creek and down the bank. Only a tiny stream of water trickled over the sandy bed. Lydia knelt for a closer look. *Someone's been poking around in the sand, digging a shallow hole, and throwing up a pile of pebbles. Or maybe it isn't a someone. Maybe it's an animal doing this—a muskrat or an otter?*

Lydia thought longingly of the friendly little flickertail squirrels back in North Dakota. Some of them had been like pets to her, and it made her sad to realize that she hadn't seen a single flickertail here in Colorado.

7

Smoke Clouds and Backfires

For two days the wind kept blowing from the north, and Father kept on trying to plow. One afternoon he appeared at the kitchen door and said in a low, unsteady voice, "There's a fire. It must have started when the train went through this morning."

Lydia jolted to her feet. "Is it coming this way?"

All three of the girls crowded to the window. Up from the northern horizon rolled clouds of black smoke!

"Yes, it's coming this way. The wind's still from the north. I'm going to start a fire beyond my firebreak and try to burn toward the big fire, but it won't be easy with such a wind." Father grabbed the matches and was gone.

"Can we help?" Polly called after him.

He stopped on the porch. "Wet some gunnysacks. Use them to beat out the sparks."

Polly dashed to the cellar to find sacks. Lydia and

Lisbet stared at one another. "I'm sure glad Father's here!" exclaimed Lisbet.

"But I wish Mother were here too," Lydia said in a small voice.

Armed with the wet sacks, the girls went outside. Their neighbors on both sides were starting fires too, just like Father. Joe and Jake were gone. They were helping dig the cellar for Ben's new house. Though it was possible to see far across the prairie, Ben's home was not visible from the Yoders'. Ben lived two miles away. Having first built his barn, Ben had partitioned off a section of it for the family to live in until the house could be built.

"I hope the fire doesn't get to Ben's," Lydia fretted, thinking of her two little nephews and her tiny niece, six-month-old Hannah. How frightened the children would be if a fire came their way!

Flames shot up from below the rolling smoke. Beneath the towering smoke clouds, the men looked puny and small as they rushed around to build their backfires. *Only God can save us*, Lydia thought as she clasped her hands and prayed.

"This reminds me so much of the prairie fire in North Dakota," Polly said, staring northward. "But we had better firebreaks that time, and we didn't try to burn toward the big fire."

The backfires struggled and sputtered as if fearful of the monstrous fire advancing upon them. Still, a patch of black grass was spreading outward, extending the protection of the plowed strips.

Flames shot up from below the rolling smoke.

The smoke got into Lydia's eyes, mouth, and nose. She could hardly breathe. She wasn't sure if it was because of the smoke or because of her fear, which clamped down on her heart like a giant fist.

"The fire is veering to the west!" Polly called above the crackle of the flames. "Has the wind changed? Or is it all because of the backfires?"

With all the smoke, it was hard to tell what direction the wind was blowing, but Polly was right. The big fire had changed direction and was now roaring down a stretch of prairie where no buildings lay in its path of destruction. It was far enough away that no sparks flew into the Yoders' yard.

Father walked over to the girls. His face was black with soot, and the white streaks on his cheeks showed where the sweat had run down. "Thank God that the wind shifted a bit. I don't know if our little backfires would have done the trick without that shift."

"When will the fire stop, Father?" asked Lydia, her eyes still on the receding flames.

"Well, there's another creek between here and town. Hopefully that will do it," Father answered.

Lisbet shuddered. "What if the whole town burned?"

Before anyone could reply, they heard galloping hoofs, and there was Jake, riding wildly up the road. He pulled the horse to a stop beside Father and gasped, "Ben's barn burned down."

"His barn!" Father echoed.

"But that's where they live!" exclaimed Polly. "Are the children okay?"

Jake struggled to calm his breathing. His face was just

as black as Father's. "Nobody's hurt. The fire didn't actually touch their property. It was a spark. You know that pile of hay Ben bought from Mr. Morgan? He had stored it outside the barn in a stack, and it caught fire. Then the barn went up in flames. There wasn't a thing we could do. It happened so fast."

"But where were the children and Barbara?" Polly persisted.

"They did just as Ben told them. They sat on the pile of earth that we dug out of the cellar. The fire didn't reach them there."

Lisbet asked urgently, "Were there any animals in the barn?"

"No. The horses were in the field," answered Jake, more calmly now.

"But their things!" exclaimed Polly. "What about their furniture, their Sunday clothes—everything?"

"All gone," Jake said with a sweep of his arm. "Nothing's left but the clothes on their backs. Some of the lumber for the new house burned too."

"Oh, that nice little dress Mother made for Hannah!" Lydia said, thinking of her niece's new Sunday dress.

"And the shirts she made for the boys," Lisbet added.

"Ben could live with us until we build a house for them," Father said, deciding on the spot. "I guess I'll go over there right now."

"Can we take the wagon? We want to go too," Lisbet pleaded.

"All right."

By the time they got to Ben's, it seemed the whole community had gathered there. Barbara's parents had already offered to take the family in, and Ben had decided to accept that offer because it was closer to his place. Everybody wanted to give them clothing, blankets, and household goods.

Poor Ben looked bewildered and put a hand to his blackened forehead. "The thing is we haven't got a house to put the things in that you want to give."

Some of the bystanders chuckled. John Miller spoke up to say, "So we'll get busy building the house right now. The foundation is ready, isn't it?"

The men, looking relieved at having something to do, headed off to the site of the new house. Lydia sat on the pile of earth, her arms around little Noah and Abner. Staring at the smoldering heap of ashes that had once been the barn, she asked the three-year-old, "Was it scary?"

He nodded his head vigorously up and down, and his blue eyes grew wide. "Scary and smoky! Mother had to cough."

Lydia looked over at Barbara, who stood holding the baby while the neighbor women clustered around her. How must her sister-in-law have felt as she watched her belongings going up in smoke?

Lydia heard Barbara's voice above the others as she said, "I told myself they're just things. We're so thankful our children are safe."

And there on the pile of earth, Lydia hugged her nephews just a little tighter.

8

Clock of Life

I don't know if I can sleep tonight," said Lisbet on the evening of the fire. "Everything just keeps going through my mind over and over again."

"I keep on smelling those flames," Lydia said with a shudder.

"Well, if we can't sleep yet, I know what we could do. We could write Mother a letter and tell her all about it," Polly suggested.

"A letter? You mean she'll be gone long enough that it's worth mailing a letter to her?" Lydia asked.

"The doctor said it'll be over a week," Polly reminded her. "If we mail the letter tomorrow, it'll reach her in the hospital the next day. She'd be glad to hear from us, I'm sure."

So they began to write. Lydia told how she felt when the fire was advancing straight toward their place and how glad she was when it veered toward the west. Then she explained how Jake came galloping home with the bad news about Ben's barn. She wrote, "But they're going to have lots of stuff again because everyone wants to give them something. Even people from town want to give furniture. The storekeeper has given them fabric to make new clothes, so the women are going to be busy sewing. And the men will build their new house real quick."

How true! In just five days' time, Ben's house was ready to move into, and the three Yoder girls went over to help them.

While looking around her furnished house, Barbara said, "Why, I think I have more things now than I had before the fire."

Everyone had been so generous. Father had built a kitchen table out of lumber. Five chairs, no matter that none of them matched, appeared out of nowhere. A tiny crib for the baby and a bigger bed for the boys showed up. Someone had given the couple a mattress. Ben and Barbara were sleeping on it on the floor until Ben had time to build a bed frame.

"And you got a new house quicker this way than you would have if the barn hadn't burned down," said Polly, who was putting on her shawl and bonnet to go home. "Lisbet? Lydia, are you ready to go? We have things we should do at home yet tonight."

Lydia hurried to get her coat, and soon the three were

on their way. A cold wind was blowing as they drove homeward. Far away to the west, the sun was slipping down behind Pikes Peak, touching the snowy slopes with sunset colors. Lydia felt as if she were wrapped in a warm blanket of contentment.

If only Mother would be in the kitchen to greet them when they got home! Leaving Lisbet to help Father unhitch the team, Lydia and Polly headed for the house. Suddenly Polly stopped and grabbed Lydia's arm. "There's smoke coming from our chimney!"

Lydia took one look at the spiral of smoke and broke into a run, calling, "Mother!" even before she opened the door.

There she was, sitting close to the stove with a bandage on the side of her head. Her dear face was all rosy from the heat of the fire. Lydia ran into her arms, and Mother held her as if she were just five years old instead of ten. "I missed you, Lydia," she murmured.

"And I missed you too! You were gone a long time."

"Just a little over a week, but a lot happened to you while I was gone."

"How did you get home?" Polly asked.

"Catherine and I took the train to town and walked to the doctor's office, which is near the station. The doctor offered to bring us home after he finished seeing his patients. When we got closer to home, we saw that all the grass in the fields is burned, and everything is black."

Coming in just then, Lisbet said, "What did you think when you got home and there was nobody here?"

Mother smiled. "I just figured you were all over at Ben's place. I got your letter, you know. At first when I read it, I said to Catherine, 'We have to go home. We can't stay here when Ben and Barbara have lost all their belongings.' But Catherine was very firm with me. She insisted I stay in the hospital until I'd recovered enough to leave safely. She assured me that you would all manage without me."

"And we did," said Father, coming inside in time to hear the last part. "But we sure are glad to have you home!"

"How is your ear, anyway?" Polly asked, busily putting the soup on for supper.

Mother touched the bandage. "Well, it's sore from the operation, but it's not throbbing anymore. The operation took away the pressure that had built up."

"Can you hear in that ear?" Lydia asked.

"I hope so. I can't tell yet, but the doctor said the operation went well."

Father said quietly, "We have much to be thankful for."

"So can we go on with our plans to have the wedding on March twelfth?" Polly asked.

Father and Mother looked at each other. Father said, "I don't know why not. If you think we'll be ready, that is."

"I think we will, but we'll be busy," Polly replied confidently.

◇◇◇◇◇

And they were. What with cleaning the house from top to bottom and preparing food for the big meal, the Yoder household whirled with activity. Besides everyone in the community, some guests from Indiana and North Dakota would be invited as well.

Sam Peachy, meanwhile, was building a small house on his homestead. Jake and Joe, claiming they needed to get out of the women's way, went to help him nearly every day.

To everyone's surprise, a light blanket of snow lay on the ground on the morning of March twelfth. Earlier, it had seemed that spring had arrived. Several hired steam tractors had been chugging around the neighborhood and plowing down the blackened prairie grass. Now suddenly on the wedding morning, winter had returned.

Of course it didn't last long. By the time all the guests had arrived and were packed into the Yoder's house, the sun had melted most of the snow. Lydia listened eagerly as the bishop from Indiana preached. "Life is like a clock," said the bishop. "The hand goes around from birth to child-hood, from youth to marriage, from middle age to old age, and finally to death. Although we do not know when our life's clock will stop, we know that God is in control."

Soon Polly and Sam stood up to be married. How happy

they looked as the bishop pronounced the blessing upon their union. Lydia was happy for them too, yet deep inside she felt a little ache. Polly was leaving home. The hand on Polly's life clock had moved around to marriage.

9

The Den in the Stream Bank

Although he never talked to anyone about it, Joe had not forgotten his dream. He still remembered how Father had reacted when he told him about the gold that had been found in Colorado. Apparently Father wasn't impressed with the idea of searching for gold. He had declared, "We need to make an honest living from the land, not go off on a treasure hunt."

That did not keep Joe from dreaming about finding gold. He reasoned that surely Father would be pleased to have the extra money, so he planned to spend his spare time hunting for gold along the creek without letting anybody know. If he never found gold, no harm would be done. And if he did, well, it was fun to imagine how delighted everyone would be.

Finding spare time was the biggest problem. During the first few months in Colorado, there simply hadn't been any! In the beginning there were so many building projects. Then Ben's barn burned down. Next came the wedding, and then it was seeding time. Working alongside his brother and Father, Joe stayed busy from dawn to dusk.

At last one day in April, Joe saw his chance. Father had gone to town, and Jake was off helping Ben. A soft chinook wind was blowing down from the Rockies, and off in the distance, the proud shoulders of Pikes Peak butted up into the blue sky.

Joe glanced around furtively to make sure Lydia and Lisbet weren't watching before he slipped behind the barn. There beneath some scrap lumber, he had hidden his gold-seeking tools. He'd found the piece of a broken shovel and an old, rusty pan in the town dump. Stuffing both into a gunnysack, he headed for the creek.

Joe squatted down by the trickling stream. He closed his eyes and did his best to remember the pictures of gold panning in the history book. First the gold seeker would scoop up some water and gravel into the pan. Then he would twirl the pan around, letting the water and the lighter sand swish out over the rim of the pan.

Gold was heavy. That was the whole idea. The lighter stuff was supposed to float out of the pan with the water, while the heavy gold settled to the bottom and stayed there.

Round and round went Joe's pan. When all the water was gone, most of the sand was too. Only a few good sized pebbles remained.

Joe stared at the pebbles. Some were smooth, and some were jagged. Although they glistened at him from the bottom of the rusty pan, anybody could see that the glistening was only because they were wet and not because they were gold.

Joe flipped the pebbles far up the bank. One thing was sure, he wasn't going to swish the same old pebbles through his pan over and over again! He scooped up some more sand, gravel, and water. *Swish, swish, swish.*

His thoughts came freely as he worked his pan. *No gold. Not that I actually expected to find any. Well, not really. Not today, but maybe someday… It takes a lot of determination. I'll really have to keep at it—if I want to find gold, that is.*

So Joe filled pan after pan after pan. He swished the gravel and water back out again. He stared hard at the pebbles that stayed and never saw any gold. *Of course not. What was I expecting?*

After a while Joe grew tired of that spot and decided to move farther up the creek. *Maybe the gold hadn't come down this far.* He understood why creeks held gold. The gold, called a mother lode, lay hidden way down deep in the underground. From this mother lode, the gold was washed downstream by the water.

A startled muskrat peered at Joe with beady eyes, and in a flash, it was gone. Joe grabbed the exposed roots of a cottonwood and swung himself up to the door of the muskrat's home. He tried to peer into the burrow, but it was as black as midnight. The muskrat would never come back out as long as he was there.

Down he dropped to the streambed again. Gravel crunched beneath his boots as he trudged on around one bend, then another, and another.

Suddenly Joe stopped. He saw something on the opposite bank halfway hidden behind scrubby cottonwoods. It looked like a door—a wooden door—built into the overhanging stream bank! This was no muskrat's lair. Muskrats didn't have wooden doors.

Joe made a swift leap across the stream. From the water's edge, he scampered up the trampled path that led to the door. Joe grabbed the wooden handle.

Suddenly he froze. *What am I doing? I can't just go barging into someone's home!* Although the door wasn't very big, it was big enough for a human to squeeze through.

Grinning sheepishly to himself, Joe knocked on the door. What a funny feeling it was to be rapping on a door that had no house!

Nothing happened. He knocked again, harder this time. *If anybody's inside, they must be sleeping pretty soundly. Oh well, maybe nobody lives here now. Maybe someone lived here years ago, say in the time of the gold rush.*

Joe's heart beat fast. He had to see what was on the other side of this door. *If a prospector used to live here, maybe he left some useful tools.*

Joe discovered the door in the stream bank.

He tugged on the carved wooden handle, and the door swung outward easily on leather hinges. Joe gasped. In front of him was a room. A regular little room! It was dark, of course, because there could be no windows here under the stream bank. But in the shadows, he could make out a tiny table, two homemade chairs, and a cupboard. And a stove!

Joe stepped gingerly across the packed-earth floor and touched the stove. It was warm. *Somebody lives here! Somebody made porridge for breakfast and left some of it in a pot on the back of the stove. Somebody slept in that narrow bed at night, covering himself with a red woolen blanket.*

Suddenly Joe couldn't get out of there fast enough. *I'm trespassing in someone else's house! What if the person comes back right now and catches me here?*

In two giant steps, he reached the door, slipped outside, and slammed it shut. He scooped up his pan and shovel and scrambled up the bank. Not caring that he trampled on the new, green shoots of wheat, he dashed across the field as if a bear were after him.

When he was almost home, Joe stopped and threw himself down in the grass. He needed time to think this over. *What am I going to do with this discovery? Should I tell Father and Mother?*

Even though he wasn't sure why not, Joe decided he wouldn't tell. *Not right now, anyway. Maybe I'll go there again, scout around, and find out some more about the mysterious little den. In the meantime, I'll just keep the whole thing a secret. It all seems a little like a dream, anyway.*

Lying there in the grass, watching the white clouds drift by overhead, Joe suddenly remembered. Last fall when he'd come to Colorado with Father to look at the land, he'd seen something that looked like a man's foot disappearing in the bushes. *Maybe that foot belonged to the owner of this den in the creek bank!*

10

A Secret Shared

Joe had a big secret, and he felt the secret weighing heavily upon his shoulders. Soon he wasn't going to be able to stand it anymore. That is how Joe Yoder felt in the days after he discovered that stream-bank home. He thought about it constantly. He wondered who lived there. More than anything else, he longed to tell someone.

Finally he decided to tell Lydia. She would enjoy sharing a secret. She often complained that he never played with her anymore. Maybe she'd feel better if he let her in on his big secret.

Lydia was outside carrying a pail of water from the well to the garden. The women seemed to be doing that a lot of the time. Practically no rain had fallen since the garden had been planted, yet Mother was determined to keep the garden thriving. And the only way to do that was to carry water.

"Here. Shall I carry that?" Joe made the offer after coming up behind Lydia.

She jumped and spilled some water. "You scared me! Look at the water we lost."

"Sorry. Water's precious, isn't it," he said, taking the pail.

"Mother is afraid that the well will go dry. It's pretty low already. The water was for the lettuce."

Joe began splashing each lettuce plant until Lydia protested. "Let me. Mother taught me how to give just enough water but not too much." Carefully she gave each little head of lettuce a measured splash.

He sat in the hot, sandy soil watching her. "You can't guess what I found along the creek the other day."

"A flickertail?" she asked without looking up.

"No. Better than that. I said you can't guess."

"Well, then gold?"

"Huh. Who wants gold? No, this is—well, it's pretty mysterious."

Lydia poured out the last drop of water and stood looking at her big brother. His yellow hair was all mussed up. Mischief twinkled in his blue eyes. "Well, if I can't guess, why don't you just tell me?"

"Either that, or I could show you," he said. "Want to go for a walk up the creek?"

She dropped the pail and answered, "Sure!"

Joe's strides were so long that she nearly had to run to

keep up with him. It made her feel a wee bit sad because it was just another reminder that Joe really wasn't her playmate anymore. What fun it was to be doing something with him once more! The farther up the creek they hiked, the more she wondered what he was going to show her. *A bird's nest maybe? But no, he'd said I couldn't guess.*

"Creek's almost dry," he commented over his shoulder. "We sure could use some rain."

"I wish it would rain for a whole week!" she replied.

He pointed to the wheat fields. "The crops don't look too good." Some of the small green plants were turning yellow, nearly the color of the parched soil. "Father says it reminds him of the first year they were in North Dakota. It was pretty dry that year too."

"I hope we get rain. I'm so tired of watering the garden."

Joe stopped so suddenly that she nearly ran into him. "There. Do you see it?"

At first she noticed nothing unusual—just some crooked cottonwoods sprouting at odd angles from the bank. Then she saw it. "A door! Right in the bank!"

"Shhh!" he said with a finger to his lips. "Maybe somebody's home today."

Lydia watched as Joe went up to the door and knocked. "Who would live in a stream bank?"

"I have no idea. There was nobody here when I found the place, but it is definitely somebody's home. I'll show you." Having knocked three times without receiving an answer, he pulled open the door.

Lydia gasped when she saw the snug interior. "It's like a playhouse! Do you think it is one?" she asked, utterly charmed.

Joe shook his head. "Can't be. That stove is real. I touched it the last time, and it was hot. Somebody had cooked porridge."

She clasped her hands. "Can we go in?"

"Better not. We'd be trespassing. We really shouldn't be standing here spying on somebody else's place." He shut the door and looked all around. "Still nobody in sight. Let's cut across the field to get home."

Joe walked more slowly so Lydia could keep up easily. "Have you told Father about this place?" she asked her brother.

"No. I figured I'd keep it a secret, but then I decided to tell you."

"You mean I'm not to tell Lisbet—or Mother?"

He stuffed his hands deep into his trouser pockets. "I guess a fellow needs to enjoy a secret sometimes."

Lydia felt troubled. "But why wouldn't we tell?"

Head down, Joe stepped carefully across the rows of new wheat. "Just because. Maybe we'll tell later on, but for now it's between you and me. I wouldn't have told you if I didn't think you could keep a secret."

That did it. If he'd trusted her, it was her duty to guard the secret. But she still felt troubled about it.

Joe's mind was already busy with something else. "I'm going to ask Father if I'm old enough to use the shotgun on my own now. That way I could go off hunting for rabbits and pheasants and other small game. We need the meat, and I'd have an excuse to check on that den in the creek bank every now and then." Joe didn't tell Lydia that it would also give him an opportunity to pan for gold.

With the crops looking so poor, Joe was more determined than ever to keep on panning. *Yes, Father thinks we should make an honest living by farming; but what if that's not possible this year? Surely nobody will despise a little gold if I find some.*

To Joe's delight, Father gave him permission to use the shotgun. Now he had an excuse to hike along the creek. He kept his pan and shovel hidden behind a rock, and nearly every day he would pan for gold for a while. Afterward he'd wander in the woods trying to find small game. Rabbits had been plentiful in the spring, but they seemed scarce now. Maybe the dry weather had an effect on them too.

◇◇◇◇◇

Haying time put an end to Joe's adventures for a while. "We have to make all the hay we can," Father said. "If the crops fail, we'll at least have hay for the horses and cattle."

"Do you really think the crops will fail?" Jake asked in dismay.

Father smiled, but it was a grave smile. "If we don't get rain soon—"

It seemed you couldn't talk with anyone for more than a few minutes without hearing something about the need for rain. People kept staring at the sky as if the rain would come if they stared long and hard enough.

Sunny skies were excellent for hay making, though. Father and the boys got busy cutting the meadow grass the steam tractors had left standing last spring. Once cut, they raked it into windrows. In a matter of days, it was cured, ready to load onto the wagon, and haul to the barn. When the loft was full to bursting, they made haystacks beside the barn.

Lydia was still busy carrying water, but now her job included taking water to the thirsty harvesters as well. It was amazing how much they needed to drink!

It seemed to Lydia that every day she had to let the pail farther down into the well to draw water. The water level was getting lower and lower. "Dear God," Lydia said as she lowered the bucket, "please don't let the well go dry. Please let it rain. We need water so badly."

But no rain came. Big, scary cracks began to open in the sunbaked soil, and the wheat was shriveling up.

"Mother, why doesn't God send rain?" Lydia asked one day.

Mother kept on trickling water over the bean plants until her bucket was empty. "Are you praying for rain?"

Lydia nodded shyly. "But I don't get an answer."

Mother put down the bucket and gazed out at the parched fields. "It's not wrong to pray for rain, Lydia, but we are not to pray like that without also saying, 'Thy will be done,' to God. We have no right to demand that He work a miracle for us. After all, it's normal for this part of the country to have dry spells, and we knew it when we moved here."

"Do you wish we hadn't moved here?"

Mother shook her head. "I'm wishing nothing of the sort. I'm thinking we should start counting our blessings, Lydia."

"What blessings?"

"Oh, there are so many. We have our family. We have homes. And friends. And work to do. Of course, we can't forget the greatest blessing of all—the love of God. To think He loved the world so much that He gave His Son Jesus to die for us."

Lydia took a deep breath. She felt better already.

11

The Prospector

One night it rained. Joe awoke at midnight and heard the drops drumming a beautiful tune on the shingles above him. He smiled to himself, turned over in bed, and went to sleep again.

Lydia didn't hear the rain in the night. In the morning the sun shone again, so she didn't know about the rain until she looked out the kitchen window. "The garden is muddy!" she squealed in delight. "Mother, did you know that it rained last night?"

"Yes, isn't it wonderful?"

"I'm going out there," Lydia declared. She dashed to the garden and sunk her feet into the squishy mud. The garden plants seemed to be smiling as they drank in the water.

After wiping her feet on the grass, Lydia went in for breakfast. "The mud's not very deep," she announced. "There's dust right underneath."

Lisbet told her, "The rain didn't last long. It was over after an hour, I think."

"We're thankful for every drop of rain," Mother said firmly as she put the platter of eggs on the table. "Is everybody ready to eat?"

After breakfast Joe took the shotgun and headed across the field. Deep in thought, he wondered, *Will these poor, shriveled wheat stalks be revived by the rain? Some seem to be standing up straighter, grateful for the moisture. Maybe there will be a crop after all. But hardly a good one. It just isn't possible after all that dry weather.*

Joe hadn't really planned to head for the den in the bank, but that was where his feet took him. Today he noticed a strange thing as he neared the spot. A wisp of smoke was curling up from the grass at the edge of the bank.

He strode over for a closer look. Sure enough, there was the smoke pipe jutting up through the earth. Joe grinned to himself. *Anyone who didn't know about the den would certainly be puzzled by this smokestack. Maybe they'd think a woodchuck was tending a fireplace somewhere underground.*

Joe leaned on his gun, thinking things over. *Do I have the courage to scramble down the bank and knock on the door? Obviously the owner of the den is at home today.*

But he didn't have to make up his mind because suddenly a thin, wrinkled face peered up at him from down below. The face belonged to a tiny gnarled man, smaller

77

than Joe. "Who's there?" asked the stranger in a scratchy voice that sounded as if it wasn't used very often.

The prospector was a small, odd man with a scratchy voice.

"I'm Joe Yoder," he answered politely, slipping down the bank. Wondering if it was proper to shake hands, Joe timidly stuck out his right hand.

The other's fingers felt almost like claws, they were so thin. "I'm Willie." He gestured toward the open door. "Not many people know where I live."

"I stumbled across your home last week," Joe confessed. "It's a nice little place."

"Come in." Willie led the way, pointing to one of the chairs.

Joe sat down, enjoying the earthy smell of the place. There was also an aroma of fried bacon. He wondered whether it would be polite to ask the question that was uppermost in his mind.

Again he didn't need to decide. "I'm a prospector," Willie told him, "and have been for fifty years. Came out here during the first big gold rush in 1859."

"Really?" exclaimed Joe. "I didn't think anybody who came to Colorado during the gold rush would still be alive."

Willie's eyes crinkled with laughter. "Now, now. That wasn't that long ago."

"Did you find lots of gold?" Joe asked eagerly.

This time Willie laughed out loud. "Look at me. I'm living in a hole in the ground like a rabbit, and you want to know if I found lots of gold!"

"I guess that was a silly question," Joe admitted, his face warm.

"That's okay. I didn't mean to laugh at you. As a matter of fact, I have found a bit of gold over the years. Enough to keep me alive."

"Recently? In this creek?" The eagerness was back in Joe's voice.

For an answer Willie got up and went to the cupboard. Placing a tiny wooden box on the table, he opened it and pushed it toward Joe.

The inside of the box was lined with soft blue cloth. On the bottom, glinting in the folds of blue, Joe saw a few flecks of—something. "Is that gold?" he asked in awe.

"The real thing. Found the one flake three months ago. The other could have been a year ago. It won't be long until I'll have to take this in to the bank. I need money for coffee, sugar, salt, and such things." Willie tapped the box thoughtfully. "You should feel honored that I've told you all this. Shows I figure you're an honest boy, not somebody who'll be back to steal my gold."

This time Joe felt the warmth rise to the roots of his hair. "I wouldn't even think of stealing." He paused, trying to grasp it all. "This means there really is gold in Phillips Creek!"

"Don't get excited," chuckled Willie. "As you can see, there isn't much. I'll never strike a bonanza, like Robert Womack did nearly twenty years ago at Cripple Creek."

"What's a bonanza?" Joe asked.

"When Womack found a big deposit of gold, they called it a bonanza," explained Willie. "His strike sure brought the excitement back for a while. Triggered a whole new gold rush, though not as many people came as in the rush of the fifties. Ah, those were the days. Whole families traveled across the prairies in their covered wagons, all aiming for Pikes Peak and gold. Somebody coined the phrase, 'Pikes Peak or bust!' That became the catchword of the gold seekers. Big old Pikes Peak was like a huge magnet drawing thousands of people to the West."

Joe closed his eyes and tried to picture it all—the wagon trains, booming towns, and excitement when somebody struck it rich. "I wish I'd been here in those days," he said dreamily.

Willie gave him a queer look. "Maybe you wouldn't have liked it. Things were pretty rough. I mean, for God-fearing people…"

Joe barely heard him. He was too busy dreaming about the heyday of the gold rush. "Are you going to be panning for gold today, Mr. Willie?"

The old man shrugged. "I do every day. It's my way of making a living."

"May I watch you?" Joe asked in the same eager voice.

"Sure. Nothing to see, though. It gets pretty boring." Willie grunted as he got to his feet. After placing the gold box back in the cupboard, he reached for his hat. "Pan's outside."

The old man led Joe quite a distance up the creek. "I have to keep trying new spots, you see. Sooner or later I'll need to make a new den farther upstream. That's why I don't want a real house."

Joe watched as Willie squatted down, expertly scooped up the gravel, and swished it out again. He didn't do it any differently than Joe had. Not really. But there was a certain practiced ease about his movements, the kind that comes from having done it thousands of times.

"Want to try it now?" Willie asked, offering him the pan.

Joe's hands trembled a little at the thought of a seasoned prospector watching him, but when he had finished, Willie said, "Good enough," and took the pan back.

"What's your father doing today?"

"Uh, I'm not sure. I was supposed to be out hunting for game." Quickly Joe realized the old prospector was hinting that it was time for him to go. "Thanks for showing me your house," he said, shouldering his shotgun.

Willie merely nodded. After Joe had gone a few steps, Willie called after him, "Don't let gold ruin your life."

Joe hesitated. *Now what did the man mean by that? How could gold possibly ruin anyone's life?* As far as Joe could see, finding gold would bring a big improvement for a poor farmer whose crops weren't very good.

He almost went back to ask what Willie meant but decided not to. Joe had a feeling Willie had answered enough questions for one day.

Luckily Joe managed to shoot one squirrel before it was

time to head home for dinner. Father might have wondered why he'd been gone so long if he'd brought home no game.

Joe thought about Willie and asked himself, *Why do I want to keep it a secret about Willie, anyway?* Suddenly he couldn't wait to tell Father all about the elderly prospector. Spotting Father near the barn, he ran up and said breathlessly, "There's a man living in a kind of den in the stream bank."

Father looked surprised. "In the stream bank, you say?"

"Yes. He's made himself a home underground. I don't know what he'd do if the creek got really high."

"So where is this?"

Joe told him how far upstream it was and offered to show it to him some day. Right then the thought occurred to Joe, *What if Willie tells Father about my interest in gold panning? What will Father think of that? I guess there's nothing I can do about it now.*

"He's an old man," Joe explained, "and he pans for gold."

Father's eyes seemed to bore into Joe's face. "I see. So there are still some prospectors around."

"Not many," Joe said, matching his strides to Father's as they went in for dinner. "Willie said there aren't many left."

"Well," said Father, "I hope this Willie also knows where true riches can be found."

Once again, Joe wanted to ask his father what he meant by that, but by this time, they had reached the kitchen door, and the aroma of Mother's delicious soup wafted out to greet them.

12

Father Goes Away

"Irrigation," Ben said moodily. "That's what the sugar beets should have had, but there was none available." Ben, Barbara, and the children had come to visit one Friday evening in August. Supper was over, and the children were playing outside in the dusk.

Lydia felt sorry for her oldest brother. He looked so dejected sitting there with his elbows propped on the table, and it was no wonder he felt that way. He had so looked forward to raising sugar beets in this warm, sunny climate, but the summer had turned out to be too warm and sunny. The beets were a failure.

Although many of the other crops had failed as well, some of the community's wheat and oat fields had produced enough grain to bring in the threshing machine later in the fall. Most of the grain would be needed as food for the people and livestock, and there would be little left to sell.

"The thing is," Ben said with more vigor, "I need work to do. I'm thinking of going out to Kansas where the crops are better and I can work on the threshing crew to make some money. We'll need it to get through the winter." He looked at Father.

"I see," said Father. He did not sound greatly surprised. "How long would you be gone?"

"I don't know. A month or six weeks, maybe." Ben looked at his wife. "Barbara's brother Aaron said he could come live at our place while I'm gone."

Jake spoke up eagerly, "I'd like to go too, Father! I could make some money to help us out."

Father turned to look at Jake. "I'm not sure that the threshing crews are a good environment for young boys."

"Aw, the fellows who helped with our threshing in North Dakota were nice," Jake said.

"Most of those men were Amish. From what I've heard, there's been some drinking among the crews down there. I have an idea. I think I will go myself for a few weeks. That way I can find out what it's like and whether it's okay for you to go, Jake."

Jake looked a little disappointed, but he said no more.

Meanwhile, Mother said anxiously to Father, "You're not so young anymore. Work on the threshing crew is hard."

Father smiled at her. "I would try to land one of the easier jobs. Band-cutting maybe. I do feel I need to make some money to support our family through the winter."

All this time Joe had been fidgeting in his chair. He couldn't help thinking of those little flakes of gold he'd seen in Willie's blue-lined box. *Maybe I can find some flakes like that in my own pan soon! That would solve all the family's problems, and nobody would have to go away for weeks at a time.* But Joe said nothing about all this. He just resolved to work harder than ever at his gold panning.

Two days later Jake hitched up the team to drive Father and Ben to the train station. Lydia stood at the window and watched them go. "I hope we don't have a prairie fire while they're gone," she said, fretting.

"Father says the conditions are not as dangerous now as they were in the winter," Mother reassured her. "We must trust in God. Let's not mope because Father's gone. Lydia, do you know what I thought you could do today? We're out of bread."

"Oh, bake bread," Lydia said moodily. "I'm not very good at it." Other times when she'd tried baking bread, it had turned out hard and dry.

"I'll help you if you need it. Your bread wasn't too bad last time. All you need is practice. And if your bread doesn't turn out perfect today, remember that mine doesn't always either, yet I've had nearly forty years of practice."

"You're not giving me much hope," Lydia grumbled as she pulled out the big metal mixing bowl and the flour. While mixing the flour with the lard, salt, molasses, and water, she reminded herself not to forget the yeast. Down to the basement she went to get the sourdough crock.

Such a lovely yeasty smell rose up when she lifted the lid! From this foamy, frothy mixture, she took one cupful and added it to her bread dough. Later, before returning the sourdough crock to the basement, she would have to "feed" it. The secret to making the yeast was to add a little more flour and milk whenever some was taken out. That way the mixture continued to ferment for the next week's batch of bread.

Lydia added the brown flour to her bread dough and then pummeled, turned, and kneaded it until her arms were tired. "Mother, is this good enough now?"

Mother came over and poked a finger into the dough. "Just right I believe. Now, do you remember the next step?"

"Yes. I have to cover the bowl with a cloth and put it in a warm place so the dough can rise." Draping a clean towel over the bowl, Lydia set it high up on the shelf behind the stove. "Now may I go out and play?"

"Until it's time to help with dinner," Mother told her. "The bread won't be ready to shape into loaves until after dinner."

As soon as the dinner dishes were washed, Lydia dusted one end of the table with flour and dumped her big, spongy mass of bread dough onto the floured surface. "How many loaves, Mother?"

"Six."

Using the long butcher knife, Lydia cut the dough into six parts. That was fun. Shaping the loaves was the hard part, and she asked, "Mother, will you please show me how to shape the loaves?"

Mother showed Lydia how to flatten the piece of dough and then roll it into a cylinder while tucking in the ends to form a lovely, solid loaf. It looked easy when Mother did it, but somehow Lydia's loaves never looked as nice as Mother's.

"Those are nicer than my loaves often are," Lisbet said admiringly as Lydia set them in pans and put them up on the shelf to rise again. It gave Lydia a glowing feeling of accomplishment to hear her big sister say that.

Off Lydia went into the garden with Mother to dig some potatoes. Because of the faithful watering, the potatoes had grown well enough. Although some were the size of two chicken's eggs, many were no bigger than one egg.

When that job was finished, it was time to go in and fire up the woodstove for baking. The hardest part of all was getting the oven temperature just right, so Mother showed Lydia how to use small pieces of split wood to make the fire burn extra hot at first and a little less so later.

As gently as if she were carrying a new baby, Lydia brought the round, fluffy loaves to the oven and slid them in. Oh, how she hoped the loaves would stay nice and round this time, instead of flopping into a heap the way they had last time!

Soon the aroma of baking bread filled the kitchen. Every three minutes or so, Lydia wanted to open the oven door to check on her loaves, but Mother warned her not to. "You'd be letting too much heat out of the oven," she explained.

At last the tops of the loaves were as brown as a ripe chestnut. "Are they done, Mother?" Lydia asked.

With her fingernail, Mother tapped one of the loaves. "Hear that hollow sound? That means they're baked through and through."

A beaming Lydia used two hot pads to carry the loaves from the oven to the table. Suddenly the kitchen door opened, and Jake stuck his head inside. "Where's Joe?"

"Oh, out hunting I suppose," Lydia said distractedly, bending down to get the third loaf from the oven.

"He's always hunting, and he doesn't often get anything," Jake growled, barging across the kitchen. *Bam!* He bumped into Lydia.

"Oh, Jake!" she shouted as her precious loaf flew from her hands and landed with a thud on the floor. She dashed to retrieve it. The lovely brown crust was broken and bashed in.

"You should watch where you're going," Jake snapped, heading back to the door. "Listen, I need someone to help chase the cattle. Who'll do it if Joe's gone?"

"I will," Lisbet offered sweetly.

After the other two were gone, Lydia sat gazing at her ruined loaf. "It'll never look right again," she mourned, trying to poke it back into shape.

"We can eat it anyway," Mother said. "And look at your five nice loaves."

Smiling, Lydia propped her chin on her hand. After a while she remarked, "Jake wasn't very nice. He's been like that ever since Father left, it seems."

"I think he's a bit tense with all the responsibility that's on his shoulders," Mother replied.

"I thought it's because he wishes he had gone threshing," Lydia said.

"Well, maybe that too, not that I'm excusing him for his impolite behavior. Remember what Father always says: 'Even though you may have a reason for behaving badly, that is still no excuse.'"

Lydia nodded. She had needed to hear that quite a few times already!

13

Drawn Like a Magnet

The shotgun was always set on two pegs above the kitchen door. One morning, about a week after Father had left, Joe took down the gun and went outside. Though a bank of mist still hung over the creek, the fields were bathed in early morning sunlight.

"What?" exclaimed the thirteen-year-old under his breath. "Somebody's walking in our lane. Why, it's—" He turned on his heel and dashed back into the house. "Mother! Father's walking in the lane, and it looks like his arm is all bandaged up."

Mother dropped her towel, Lisbet dropped her dishrag, Lydia dropped her broom, Joe carefully put down the shotgun, and just like that, all four of them were out the door.

Father's right arm was in a sling. He smiled when he saw all those family members spilling out of the house. He looked very, very tired as he slumped down on the porch steps and said, "I guess you're surprised to see me."

"You're hurt," Mother said, touching the sling.

"Yes. I was careless. I should have watched myself better. I cut my hand while band-cutting on the thresher and had to get it stitched up." He passed his free hand across his forehead. "Now there's a doctor's bill to pay. I should have been more careful."

"Accidents can happen," Mother said. "You should come in and lie down. Joe, please help Father on that side. I'll help him here." Between them, Father staggered through the kitchen to the bedroom and collapsed onto the bed.

"How did you get home?" Joe asked, standing near the door.

"Took the night train. Walked to the doctor's. Waited until he came out here to see a patient." Father sounded exhausted. His eyes were closed.

"You mean you got your hand stitched here in Wild Horse by Dr. Crawford?" Lisbet asked.

"No, no. There was a doctor in the town close by where we were threshing. The owner of the thresher paid the bill for me. Now I owe him."

"Don't worry about that," Mother said firmly. "You have to rest and get well. Would you like some breakfast before you sleep?"

Father opened his eyes briefly. "Breakfast sounds good. Let me see…I don't think I had supper last night either."

The rest of them had eaten breakfast an hour ago, but in minutes Mother had fried two eggs and toasted a slice of bread. After arranging this on a platter with a glass of milk, she took Father's breakfast into the bedroom.

Lisbet looked around the kitchen in a dazed sort of way. "Now, what was I doing, anyway?"

"You were washing dishes. You dropped the dish rag here on this chair," Lydia said, "and I was sweeping the kitchen."

"Poor Father," Lisbet said as she went on with the dishes. "I think he's in pain."

"I hope it's not too bad," said Lydia, picking up the broom.

Joe shouldered the shotgun once more. "I'll be off hunting now. Father would like squirrel for supper, I'm sure."

He headed straight for the creek. Tucking the gun onto the lower branches of a tree, he brought out his pan and began swishing gravel. Panning for gold seemed more urgent than ever, now that Father's plan to make money had failed. *It's up to me,* Joe told himself, making the gravel fly. *If nobody else can make money for the family, then I have to.*

Meanwhile, back home in the garden, Lydia was worrying as she helped Mother dig turnips. "I wonder why that had to happen to Father." She let out a big sigh as she snipped the top off another turnip.

Mother's answer was practical and the same one she gave Father earlier. "Accidents happen."

Lydia sat back on her heels. "But we hardly have enough money. Why would God let this happen?"

"Oh, Lydia," said Mother with a shake of her head. "Things like this happen all the time. It's true, God could have prevented it, but the Bible says that God chastens those whom He loves. When trials come our way, we need to keep on being thankful for His love. If we trust Him, something good may come from this happening."

◇◇◇◇◇

Just a few days later, something good did come along. It was Saturday morning, and with a clatter of hoofs, John Miller rode up to the Yoders' door.

Spying him from inside the window, Father eased himself out of his chair. "It looks like John doesn't want to dismount. He must have a message that he's taking 'round the community."

Lydia followed Father to the door. How surprised John looked when he saw Father! "I thought you were gone threshing," he exclaimed.

Father touched his bandaged hand. "I was. Then this happened."

"Ach, too bad. Arm broken?"

"No. I cut my hand. Needed stitches."

"I see. Well, I'm glad you're home, and you will be too when you hear my news. There's to be church at our place tomorrow. Preacher Aaron Mast arrived from Pennsylvania on the train this morning."

Father's face lit up. "That is good news indeed. Jake could hitch up the team to bring us to church. Thanks for letting us know."

"See you then." John wheeled his horse around smartly and was off to let the next family know.

To think that I would have missed hearing a visiting minister if the accident hadn't happened, Father thought as he marveled at how this all had happened.

On Sunday morning Aaron Mast stood at a spot in the Miller house where he could look out the window at Pikes Peak glistening blue and white on the horizon. "I am sure you must often think of the words in Psalm 121 as you look at the peak. 'I will lift up mine eyes unto the hills, from whence cometh my help. My help cometh from the LORD, which made heaven and earth.'

"On our way here on the train, I spoke with a man who said that this mountain seemed like a magnet during the days of the gold rush. From far across the prairies, the gold seekers used the peak to guide them to their destination."

Aaron's gaze left the window and traveled over the congregation. "Dear brothers and sisters, we must not let our hearts be drawn by a lust for earthly treasure. What an empty, hollow thing that is! There is something far better that should draw us like a magnet. In John 12:32 we read these words of Jesus: 'And I, if I be lifted up from the earth, will draw all men unto me.' Yes, Christ was lifted up from the earth on the cross, and we must look to Him for our help. Yes, our very life!"

14

Sick Man

On Monday morning Joe's shotgun hung once more in the tree while he knelt at the water's edge with his pan. Joe panned—unsuccessfully, as usual—until the sun had crept up toward the top of the sky. Then he grabbed the shotgun and set off upstream. Today he was lucky. He shot a partridge and a squirrel in less than half an hour.

Slinging the game over his shoulder, he headed downstream again until he caught sight of the door of the prospector's den. *Why not pop in and see if he's at home?* Joe thought, realizing he hadn't seen the old man for a while.

Knock, knock. Joe waited. No sound from within. He knocked again. He was just about to turn away when he heard a weak voice say, "Come in."

Joe frowned. *Is that Willie's voice? In a way it sounds like him, and yet it doesn't.*

He pulled open the door and allowed the sunlight to spill into the shadowy little room.

The old man lay on the bed, a blanket drawn up partly over his face. Even from the doorway, Joe could see that Willie was shivering. "Is something wrong?" Joe asked, going over to the bed.

Willie's teeth chattered so badly that he could barely speak. "G-guess I h-have a c-cold or something. A b-bit f-feverish."

Alarm shot through Joe. How thin Willie's face was! The skin was stretched like white paper over the cheekbones. "Have you been sick for a while already?"

"I d-don't know," admitted Willie. "M-maybe a f-few days."

Joe offered quickly, "Shall I go for help?"

Such a strange look came into Willie's faded eyes! It reminded Joe of the look he sometimes saw in a wild animal's eyes when it was cornered and couldn't escape.

"Oh, well, I d-don't know," he stammered.

Joe made up his mind. "I'll go get Father, but before I go, shall I put this other blanket on you?"

Willie actually managed a smile of gratitude as Joe spread the green woolen blanket over him. Apparently he had been too sick to get it himself, even though it was at the foot of the bed.

Forgetting the game he'd shot, Joe loped across the grain stubble. He hoped Father would be able to go and see Willie. Father had seemed quite well yesterday, but this morning he had been very tired again. "Seems it takes all my strength to heal this wound," Father had remarked with a wan smile. It made Joe wonder just how bad that cut was underneath those bandages.

He found Father sitting at the kitchen table. "Willie's sick," Joe announced. "Real sick. Looks like he hasn't been out of bed much for a few days."

"Willie," repeated Father, as if he couldn't think who that was. "Oh, you mean the prospector who lives in the creek bank. I never did get around to visiting him."

"Well, he's very sick," Joe said again urgently.

Father looked at him. "From what you say, I'd guess someone should go for the doctor. In the meantime, someone should go to Willie as well. Maybe I could do that if Jake would agree to go after the doctor."

"Is it far to the den?" asked Mother.

"Not terribly far," Joe answered.

"Well, I'll go along," decided Mother.

"Joe, will you ask Jake to go get the doctor? He can ride King. Then please show us where Willie lives."

Jake was forking straw in the barn. He listened to Joe's story, asked a few questions, saddled King, and set off. Meanwhile, Father and Mother had started slowly across the field with Lydia trailing after them. Joe could easily catch up. In fact, he found it hard to walk slowly enough for Father.

They eventually arrived at the door in the riverbank. Father nearly stumbled over Joe's pan and asked, "What's this?"

"Oh, that's to pan for gold," Joe mumbled.

"Oh. Well, Joe, will you go in first, since he knows you?"

Joe knocked. As soon as he heard Willie's voice, he went in and stood near the bed. "I brought my parents here. They want to help you."

Again Willie's face got that look. He pulled the blanket up higher as Father and Mother approached the bed. "Leave me alone," he begged.

Father told him kindly, "We just want to help."

Mother quickly made a fire in the stove. Finding the oatmeal, she stirred together a thin gruel and brought it to Willie. "Here's something for you to eat."

Willie stared at the bowl. Finally he reached out a claw like hand that shook badly. Anybody could see that he wasn't able to hold the bowl, much less handle a spoon.

Father helped Willie hold up his head, while Mother dribbled the gruel into his mouth, a few drops at a time. Lydia watched wide-eyed from the door. She had never seen such a sick person.

After a while Father stuck his head out the door. "Where's Joe? Oh, there you are. You'd better go back to the house. When the doctor comes, someone will have to tell him where Willie is."

Father helped Willie hold up his head,
while Mother dribbled the gruel into his mouth.

"Okay,"

Lydia scrambled up the bank after Joe, but he trotted so fast that she couldn't keep up. She wanted to beg him to wait, but she knew he should hurry. What if the doctor was already there at the house?

Sure enough, Dr. Crawford's car came bumping toward

Lydia across the field. Joe grinned at her from the passenger side. Getting a ride in a car wasn't something that happened often to the Yoder family.

Lisbet was full of questions when Lydia finally reached the house, so she told her all she knew. Soon they saw the doctor's car coming back, more slowly this time. "He's probably got the sick man in the car, so that's why he's driving carefully," Lisbet surmised.

Joe loped along beside the car, and last of all came Father and Mother. Father trudged ever so slowly. Mother supported him by holding onto his good arm. As soon as he reached the kitchen, Father dropped into a chair.

"Is Dr. Crawford taking Willie to the hospital?" Lydia asked.

"For now he'll just take him to Mrs. Whitsun's boarding house. He wants to make some inquiries and find out if Willie has relatives nearby. He thinks Willie may just have the flu," Mother replied. "We offered to take him into our house, but Dr. Crawford said he'd rather take him to town."

"He thought," Father put in with a wry smile, "that we already have enough sick people the way it is."

15

The Miller Boys

Once Father's hand was better, Jake finally got his wish to go to work on a threshing crew. On the morning he was to leave, Father read from Proverbs 3.

> My son, forget not my law; but let thine heart keep my commandments...Let not mercy and truth forsake thee: bind them about thy neck; write them upon the table of thine heart...Trust in the LORD with all thine heart; and lean not unto thine own understanding. In all thy ways acknowledge him, and he shall direct thy paths.

Closing the Bible, Father said to Jake, "The crew you will be joining is quite decent, but there are a few fellows who are mainly out for a good time. With God's help, may you resist temptation and stand strong in the faith."

Jake nodded very seriously. He didn't seem to know what to say.

Lydia felt a lump forming in her throat as she watched her big brother pick up his bag and start toward the door. "Goodbye! See you soon," she called to him.

"See you," Jake echoed back to her.

"I'll be back in a month or so. There's Samuel Miller coming up the road now with Jonas." With that he stepped outside and closed the door behind him. Jonas was Jake's age, and he too was going to join the threshing crew. His father had agreed to drive the two young men to the train station.

Lydia ran to the window and said, "Maybe Rebecca and Veronica came along to visit me while their father is in town." When no girls climbed down from the wagon when it stopped to pick up Jake, Lydia said sadly, "They haven't been here for quite a while."

"I know what," began Mother. "When Samuel comes back, we'll try to stop him. We'll ask him if they could come for Sunday dinner."

"Yes, let's," cried Lydia. "May I bake a cake? I'd like to make a pumpkin cake."

"That's a good idea!"

Everything worked out fine. Lydia saw Samuel Miller

when he was still quite a distance down the road, so they had plenty of time to intercept him. He was sure his family would like to come on Sunday, so Lydia and Lisbet got busy with preparations. They cleaned the house, peeled potatoes, and stewed fruit besides baking a pumpkin cake.

The Yoders' table ended up being quite crowded that Sunday. Thinking that Barbara must be feeling lonely with Ben gone, Mother invited her and the children too. Of course they thought of Polly and Sam and invited them as well. What with the Millers' four children and the Yoders' three, that made seventeen people!

Joe knew exactly what he wanted to do with the Miller boys. "Would you like to see the prospector's house in the creek bank?" he asked as the boys went outside after dinner.

"Sure thing," said fourteen year-old Israel, and, of course eleven-year-old Levi agreed.

They reached the den in record time. "Willie's not home yet," Joe told the other two. "I guess he's still sick."

"In the hospital?" Levi asked.

Joe shrugged. "I don't know. To tell you the truth, we haven't heard from him since Dr. Crawford took him away. Maybe he's gone to live with relatives. He was pretty old to be living alone."

"You know, I wouldn't have noticed this little door if I'd just walked by," Israel said admiringly. "It's like a secret hideaway."

Levi asked eagerly, "Can we go in?"

"Father said we're not to go in, but we may open the door and peek inside," Joe pushed the door open, and they all crowded close to take a look.

"Everything is so tiny. Willie must not be a big man," remarked Israel.

"No, he's not even as tall as I am," Joe replied.

"It would be fun to go in and sit on those chairs," Levi said wistfully.

"Father said we're not to," Joe said again. Soon he shut the door and suggested, "Shall we sit on the opposite bank?"

The stream was so narrow that they could easily hop across. On the sun-warmed sand of the bank, they found a good spot to sit. Israel announced, "We've seen the teacher, Miss Price."

"Oh? We heard that school's to begin soon, but we didn't know if the teacher had arrived," Joe said.

"We went with Father to help get the school ready. You probably heard that they're fixing up the Higgins's shed. It's really quite a nice classroom now. And the teacher will board at the Higgins's house. Miss Price is tiny. Smaller than I am."

"Oh?" Joe said again, noting that Israel was a good inch shorter than he was.

"And not very old. Maybe not much older than I am. Well, maybe as old as your sister Lisbet." Israel said with a grin. "Do you think Miss Price can make us listen?"

Joe shifted uncomfortably. He wasn't sure what he should say to that.

Israel got to his feet. "I'm going to take another peek at that prospector's cave." With a single leap, he was across the creek and at the door. To Joe's distress, he pulled it open and disappeared inside.

Levi followed his brother into the den. Joe hopped over and stood unhappily outside the door. How he wished he hadn't brought the Miller boys here! What if they damaged some of Willie's belongings?

Israel was walking stoop-shouldered around the low room, poking into every corner. He opened the stove lid. He got down on his hands and knees and peered under the bed. "I'm looking to see if he left any gold lying around," he explained to Joe. "He did pan for gold, didn't he?"

"Uh, yes," stammered Joe. How could he get these boys out of here before they started nosing into the cupboard?

Just then Israel reached for the cupboard door. Joe opened his mouth to tell him not to touch that cupboard, but shut his mouth before any words came out. If he said anything, Israel would certainly wonder what was inside.

"Here's a little wooden chest! Maybe this is where he keeps his gold," Israel said.

Joe clenched his fists. He wanted to go over and wrench the little blue-lined box out of Israel's hands.

Israel dumped the box upside down on the table. "Huh.

It's empty. Well, Levi, we better get out of here. Joe doesn't look too happy with us, does he?"

Joe bit his lip as they passed him. He wanted to go in there and check whether those little flakes of gold lay on the table. It was possible Israel just hadn't seen them. But, of course, it wouldn't work for him to do that now, so Joe closed the door carefully and followed the other two up the bank.

For Joe the afternoon had been spoiled. He tried to be friendly and think of something else he and the boys could do together, but nothing was fun anymore. They ended up sitting on the lawn near Father and Samuel, who had taken two chairs outdoors to sit and visit. How relieved Joe was when the Millers left for home!

There was no time to sneak off and set Willie's home to rights that evening because Joe had to do the chores. Father did his best to help feed the cattle, but he still couldn't use his right hand.

It wasn't bandaged any more, and the wound had healed quite nicely, but there was a vivid scar across the palm, and Father couldn't move his fingers very much. He had explained to Joe that the nerves were probably damaged.

Tonight, after feeding some grain, Father sat on a low wall and watched Joe forking hay. "What did you boys do this afternoon?" he asked.

Joe stopped forking hay. "We went to see Willie's house."

"I see." Father paused and then asked quietly, "What happened? You didn't seem too happy after you came back."

"They went inside," Joe blurted out. "I told them not to, but they didn't listen."

"I see. Was anything damaged?"

"I don't think so, but they messed around. I plan to go and put things right."

"That's good. I might go with you tomorrow. I should talk with Samuel about this. If boys are allowed to do something wrong without being chastised, their consciences get hardened, and that is not what we want for our boys." Smiling at Joe, he continued to say, "We want your conscience to be tender and willing to make things right."

Joe smiled too. He was glad to hear that Father would go with him to the den.

◇◇◇◇◇

As soon as the chores were done the next morning, they walked across the field.

"I wonder how Willie is," Father said.

"How can we find out?" Joe asked.

"I guess we could ask Dr. Crawford."

When they reached Willie's place, Joe went in and straight to the table. "There they are!" he said, pointing to three tiny flakes of gold gleaming beneath the overturned box.

Father bent for a closer look. "Gold?"

"Yes. Israel, he-he said he was checking to see if Willie left any gold. He dumped this box, but he didn't even see the gold."

"He didn't realize the pieces would be this small. Had Willie showed you the gold?"

Joe felt his face grow warm. "Yes, he did. He trusted me. Now this happened."

"Well, the gold is still safe." Carefully Father nudged the tiny flakes back into the blue-lined box. "I think we had better talk to Dr. Crawford. This gold might help to pay Willie's medical bills."

"Gold is worth a lot, isn't it?" Joe said as they walked home again. "Even little pieces like that can pay doctor bills."

Father gave him a strange look and then slowly quoted, "'Love not the world, neither the things that are in the world. If any man love the world, the love of the Father is not in him… And the world passeth away, and the lust thereof: but he that doeth the will of God abideth forever.'"

16

Miss Price and the Boys

I wish I could go with you," Lisbet admitted to Lydia on the first day of school.

Lydia laughed as she picked up her lunch bucket. "That would be fun, but why would you want to go back to school when you're eighteen already?"

"Maybe because you have such a young teacher," Lisbet answered.

Lydia laughed again. "She's no older than you are, so she could barely be your teacher." She looked out the window. "Joe's still in the barn. I hope he won't mind if I start off without him. I don't want to be late."

"Maybe I should have done some of his chores this morning," said Lisbet. "Oh, there he comes now."

"He sure isn't walking very fast, and to think that he still needs to wash up and change into his good clothes," fretted

Lydia. Brushing past her brother on the walk, she told him saucily, "You better hurry."

"Why?" Joe shot back.

"Miss Price will mark you tardy."

"So what?"

That stopped Lydia in her tracks. "Don't you even care about being on time on the very first day of school?"

"Oh well," replied Joe with a shrug, "I'll get there."

Lydia swished off down the road. *Why's Joe acting so stodgy today? Doesn't he care what the new teacher thinks of him?*

She met the two Kanagy children just as they came out of their house. Little Aaron and Amanda were glad to have Lydia's company on the way to school. To them, she was a big girl, even though she was only eleven.

Aaron and Amanda chattered nonstop all the way to school. This was going to be Aaron's first day of school, and he certainly was excited. "I can count to one hundred," he told Lydia, "and I can read."

"Not much," scoffed his eight-year-old sister. "Just ten words."

Unabashed, Aaron went on to list all the words he could read: dog, cat, mother, father, and so forth. Lydia listened and smiled. It was fun being with someone so enthusiastic about school. In the back of her mind, she still fretted about Joe being late.

All that worrying was useless because Joe came

sauntering through door just as the bell rang. By that time Miss Price had already organized the classroom. Most of the thirty-five children had been told where to sit.

Miss Price eyed Joe as he entered the classroom. "There are still two missing. Isn't there another Miller boy, and another Higgins boy?"

Levi Miller raised his hand. "Israel had to help Father this morning."

Miss Price's eyes narrowed. "He's not coming?"

Levi shrugged. "I think he is."

Just then there was a banging on the porch. In popped the two oldest students—Israel Miller and Anton Higgins, both fourteen years old. Lydia felt a little shiver pass through her. They seemed to tower over the teacher.

Miss Price was not fazed. She calmly showed the boys their seats.

Because they were given seats quite a distance apart, Anton raised his hand and said, "Aren't all the eighth graders supposed to sit together?"

Miss Price gave him a look that seemed to say that he was being impudent, but all she said was, "This is the way I've planned the seating."

As Anton slumped down in a disagreeable way, Lydia shivered again. *Why does it seem like a cold draft entered the room along with those two big boys? What if they caused trouble for the teacher?*

Miss Price moved on with her schedule. She introduced

the opening exercises and gave the students a quick talk on the school rules. Then she passed out books and started the first classes.

Miss Price stepped up to the chalkboard and began the lesson.

Seated at the very end of the third row, Lydia could easily see all three of the big boys—Joe, Israel, and Anton—without turning her head. How she hoped they would behave! Every now and then, she saw Israel and Anton smiling at each other. She did not like the way those smiles looked.

It happened in math class. Anton wadded up a ball of paper and flipped it across the row. It landed squarely on Israel's desk. Israel grinned and began unfolding the paper.

"Anton." Miss Price's voice cut the air like steel. "Go to that corner and stand with your back turned to the classroom. Stay there until I tell you to go back to your desk."

Anton blinked in surprise. He waited a few seconds, but Miss Price's gaze never wavered. She stood still with her hands on her hips.

Finally he got to his feet, half lifting the desk with his knees as he did so. The soles of his shoes made a scraping noise as he walked across the bare, wooden floor. Lydia didn't dare turn her head to watch him head for the corner, but when Miss Price relaxed and went back to the first-grade math class, Lydia knew that Anton must have obeyed.

Lydia tried very hard not to let the incident spoil her day, but she simply could not understand why it had happened. *Why did the boys want to give our new teacher a hard time? And on the very first day of school?*

That night in the barn, Lydia blurted out her question to Joe. "Why did Israel and Anton act like that?"

Joe was carrying the lantern over to the pigpen but stopped when he heard the question. The lantern cast a glow over his face as he answered slowly, "I don't know."

"Miss Price has to work hard to teach so many children," Lydia went on reproachfully. "Why would anyone want to make trouble for her?"

"I don't know," Joe said again, still standing there with the lantern. After a while he added, "A week ago Israel was talking about how he might try out the new teacher."

"Oh," said Lydia, thinking that over. "Is that why you weren't enthused about going to school this morning?"

"Maybe," said Joe as he moved on to the pigpen.

"Trouble at school?" Father asked, suddenly appearing out of the shadows.

Lydia's face grew warm when she realized he had been listening. Not that she'd said anything to be ashamed of, but she felt uncomfortable about Father finding out about the actions of those two boys. "Anton threw a paper to Israel," she explained. Saying it like that made it sound like a small thing. Too small to call trouble.

"He was being disrespectful," Father said.

"Yes," replied Lydia, relieved that he understood. "So was Israel."

"Anybody else?" Father's eyes went to the glow of the lantern over by the pigpen where Joe was busily forking straw.

Lydia shook her head. "Not Joe."

"We want to teach our children how important it is to obey. It's the only way to have God's blessing." Father's voice sounded a little strange, as though something was caught in his throat.

Father cleared his throat and moved a few steps toward Joe to make sure he could hear. "Dr. Crawford stopped me on the street today to talk about Willie."

"You mean you were in town?" Joe asked. "I thought you couldn't drive yet with that hand."

"I caught a ride with Reuben Kanagy," Father explained. "Anyway, the doctor said Willie is out of the hospital now, though he was pretty sick for a while."

"But he isn't back in his home?" asked Lydia.

"No, he's living with his brother over at Ordway. Willie sent a letter to Dr. Crawford to tell him about the gold in that box and how he wants to pay his hospital bill. The doctor plans to stop in here sometime soon to pick up that little box."

"Shall I go get it first thing tomorrow morning?" Joe quickly offered.

"That would be a good idea."

The next morning Joe was out of bed at the crack of dawn. Taking the shotgun in case he met a squirrel, he strode toward the creek. Little by little the sun peeped over the horizon, until finally the light touched Pikes Peak, far away on the western horizon.

Hastily Joe grabbed his pan and scooped up some gravel. This was another reason why he wasn't too enthused about school starting. There was no more time for his treasure hunt.

He stared at the pebbles, hoping to see a gleaming fleck or even a nugget, but there was nothing. As Joe tossed out the gravel, he remembered what Father had said the other Sunday evening: "We want your conscience to be tender, willing to make things right." Last night Joe had overheard Father say to Lydia that the only way to have God's blessing was to be obedient.

Slowly Joe put the pan back in its hiding place. *Am I being obedient if I keep on panning for gold in secret without Father's approval? Am I any better than boys like Israel and Anton who disobey openly?*

Joe ducked down and entered the low doorway of Willie's house. There in the cupboard was the little box. Joe opened it and stared at the gleaming gold.

But I only hunt for gold because I want to help Father, Joe argued with himself. Tucking the box under his arm and picking up the shotgun, he started for home. It was high time to help with the chores.

17

Storm Dog

Jake came walking in from Wild Horse one October evening. His face was as brown as a nut beneath his tumbled red hair. It seemed to Lydia that he had grown taller and wider too. His arms rippled with muscles when he took off his jacket. "I must have pitched a million sheaves," he told the girls with a grin.

"What about Ben? And Jonas? Are they back too?" Mother asked

"Yep. Threshing is over for this year, at least for that crew. What's for supper, Mother?"

"Potato and turnip soup along with some dried corn," answered Mother.

"Mmmmm. Sounds good and smells even better." Jake sat down at the end of the table in his usual spot.

Scurrying to set the table for supper, Lisbet asked, "Why are you so hungry? I thought they made big meals for threshers."

"Well, yes, but…" Jake paused. He wasn't used to making a fuss about things. "I guess I'm ready for home cooking again."

For Lydia that answered a question she hadn't dared to ask. Jake was glad to be home. Sometimes she had worried about him while he was in Kansas. After all Father had made it sound like there was a danger of falling into bad company.

"You came just in time," Father informed Jake. "We've run out of coal. Joe and I were wondering whether we could go and get some on our own, but Joe is supposed to go to school, and I'm not much good at driving or handling a shovel for that matter."

Jake's eyes went to Father's hand. "Still not well?"

Father shook his head. "No, but it's coming. Very slowly."

◇◇◇◇◇

So the very next day, Father and Jake went off to the coal mines, twenty miles away, where all the families dug their own coal. More fuel was needed right away. The nights were growing colder now that November was almost here.

But winter never came in 1910, at least not the kind of winter Lydia had known in North Dakota. There was no snow. Throughout January 1911, the mild, sunny weather stayed on.

At last one morning in February, Lisbet woke Lydia with a little shriek. "Snow! Lots of it!"

In a flash Lydia joined her at the window. The pane was so plastered with snow that she could barely see outside. In the swirling whiteness, the dim shape of the barn was just visible. "Why, it's a blizzard!" Lydia exclaimed.

Lisbet didn't agree to that. "Have you forgotten the North Dakota blizzards? Remember how the wind used to pound the house? You couldn't see a thing outdoors."

"Well, yes, but this is almost as good," Lydia said while putting on her shoes. "I wonder if I have time to go outside before breakfast."

When she entered the kitchen, however, she heard the men stamping snow off their boots on the porch. Apparently they had finished the morning chores already.

Joe's coat was all frosted with snow when he burst in and said, "Do you know what, Lydia? There's a dog out there."

"A what?" she exclaimed in disbelief.

"A dog. In the barn," Joe repeated.

"Is it a nice dog? Not wild?"

"I don't know if it's nice. It looks pretty sick to me. It's just lying in the hay with its head between its paws. Hardly paid any attention to us while we were doing chores,"

"Poor dog. Maybe it got too cold in the storm, and it came to our barn for shelter," said Lydia. She wanted to run out through the snow right away, but she couldn't because everyone was sitting down for breakfast.

Half an hour later, Lydia eagerly pulled on her coat. "I have time to go see the dog before I have to get ready for school, don't I Mother?"

"Yes, but…" Mother looked at Father. "You'll go out with her? We don't know anything about this dog."

Father nodded and got his hat and coat. Already the snow had stopped, and the sun was shining. What a dazzling world! The drab brown prairie had been transformed into a winter wonderland.

Lydia didn't spend much time enjoying the scenery, though. She had to see that dog. For years she had wished to have one. Now, maybe her wish was coming true!

The dog's coat was black—a dull and patchy black. The moment she saw him, Lydia felt sure that his fur had once been gleaming and thought she could probably get it to gleam again.

The dog raised his head when he saw Lydia. His tail thumped three times on the hay. Then his head went down again, and the tail lay still. Lydia knelt beside him, murmuring, "You poor dog. You're all worn out and probably hungry. Just look at your ribs sticking out."

Father stood looking down at the two. "Shall I bring him some milk?"

"Please!" By this time Lydia was stroking the dog's head. The dog gave a little sigh, as if to say, *Now I've found someone who likes me.*

Lydia fed the poor, tired dog a bowl of milk.

When Father brought the milk, Lydia shoved the bowl right under the dog's black nose. How eagerly he slurped it up! As though the milk had given him strength already, he staggered to his feet. After a few seconds, though, he flopped down again.

"I have to go," Lydia told the dog reluctantly. "Will you bring him some more milk at noon, Father?"

Father smiled. "I guess I could."

With wings on her feet, Lydia hurried to school. She could hardly wait to tell the other girls about her dog. They were suitably impressed and asked all sorts of questions. Lydia didn't know all the answers, but one thing she did know was that the dog's name would be Storm Dog because the snowstorm had brought him.

Apparently Joe told the boys about the dog too. During the lunch hour, Anton Higgins teased Lydia about the tramp she was taking in. Israel chimed in with a taunt about girls who didn't know a dog from a coyote.

Lydia flounced away from the big boys without saying a word, even though she felt like telling Anton, "That dog's a lot nicer than you are!"

Actually Anton had been behaving pretty well for the last little while. For weeks he had kept doing little things to make life miserable for the teacher, but Miss Price never backed down. Firmly and consistently she punished him when he did wrong—just as she did with any of the students. With Anton it had finally paid off. Though he would never be a model student, he had learned a lot. The funny thing was that anybody could see that deep down he really did like his teacher.

◇◇◇◇◇

By the next day, a warm chinook wind blew down from Pikes Peak. The snow melted fast and turned the fields into mud. Torrents of brown water ran down to the creek.

"I wonder what the creek looks like!" Joe said to Lydia on their walk home from school. "Maybe it'll overflow the banks. I'm going to have a look."

Lydia wasn't interested. "I have to see how Stormy's doing." Already she had shortened the dog's name to Stormy. She turned in at the barn even before going to change her clothes.

Joe changed in record time. Grabbing a cookie, he told Mother that he wanted to check out the creek before chore time. "I'm wondering if Willie's den is flooded," he explained.

Mud sucked at his boots as he crossed the fields. By the time he reached the creek bank, his boots had grown to twice their normal size.

When he saw the stream, Joe forgot about his boots. Was this the same quiet, meandering creek where he'd spent hours panning for gold? Wild and brown, the current tore down between the banks as if it couldn't wait to reach the river. The water was nearly halfway up the bank!

After locating Willie's chimney, Joe carefully let himself down the bank while hanging onto the bushes. Sure enough, the water lapped at the bottom of Willie's door. Joe sloshed it open. Water had spread across the floor, eddying around the legs of the table and chairs, but so far nothing had been damaged.

"If the water goes down soon, things should be okay," Joe muttered as he pulled himself to the top of the bank again.

Suddenly he thought of something. *Where's my gold pan? The last time I used it, about a week ago, I wedged it between the exposed roots of that one certain cottonwood partway up the bank.*

Joe walked along the creek until he reached the spot. He was pretty sure this was the spot because at the edge of the swirling water, he could see those gnarled roots. But he saw no rusty old pan. It must have been torn from its hiding place and carried downstream by the swift current.

Joe turned his back and headed for home. "Good riddance," he said under his breath.

18

Set Free

With the arrival of spring, new hope poured into the hearts of the farmers who had watched last year's crops wilt away. Steam tractors were hired to break more land. They chugged around the neighborhood, spewing clouds of smoke and steam.

"May I go closer to watch Mr. Baumgartner, Mother?" Lydia asked on the day the tractor came to their farm.

"Yes, but stay out of his way," Mother warned.

"I will," Lydia promised. "Here, Stormy!"

The black dog scampered up to her, pushed his head under her hand, and begged to be petted. His coat was shiny now, and his ribs no longer showed.

"Let's go to the field," Lydia told him. He bounced away ahead of her, always ready for a gopher hunt. That was what a walk in the fields meant to Stormy. Nothing was more fun than chasing gophers back into their burrows.

While Lydia stood watching the big steam tractor turning over the soil, Stormy yapped at any gophers he saw. Suddenly his bark changed into a kind of puzzled *yip-yip*.

Lydia hurried over to him. His nose was down to the ground. There in the grass, lay a quivering bundle of black and white feathers.

"A bird!" Lydia scooped it up in her hands. She could feel the violent beating of a tiny heart. Something was wrong with one of the bird's wings.

"Did the tractor hurt your wing?" she murmured to the tiny creature. "I'll take you home. As soon as your wing gets well, you can fly again."

Back at the house, Lydia told Mother, "I've found a bobolink." How well she remembered the high, ecstatic trilling of the bobolinks above the fields of North Dakota!

Mother peered into Lydia's cupped hands. "Hmmm. It does look like a bobolink. It's the first one I've seen in Colorado. How did you manage to catch it?"

"Oh, it can't fly. I think the steam tractor must have hurt it. Can I keep it in the barn until its wing heals?"

"I suppose so, but you'll have to put it in a box, or Greasy the cat will eat your bobolink for supper."

"What? A bobolink?" asked Joe, coming in just then.

"Yes, a lame one. I'm going to help it get well," Lydia told him. "His name is Bobby."

Joe grinned. "First Stormy, then Bobby. You're gathering quite a menagerie."

"What's a man-ash-ry?" Lydia asked.

"Oh, it's a collection of animals. Pretty soon we'll have a zoo on our farm."

Undaunted by her brother's teasing, Lydia set to work making Bobby comfortable. She used a wooden packing box to make a cage. Across the opening she tacked a piece of screen that was left over from building the screen door. She gave Bobby some hay to sit on and some grain to eat.

At supper time, when Mr. Baumgartner was eating with the Yoder family, Mother mentioned the bobolink to Father. Mr. Baumgartner spoke up. "I doubt if it's a bobolink. You don't see those around here."

"So there must be another bird that's black and white and yellow like a bobolink," Mother said.

Mr. Baumgartner nodded. "Ever heard of lark buntings? They're common around here. Could I see the bird you found?"

"Of course," said Mother. "Lydia will show it to you. She has it in the barn."

Lydia felt her face grow warm. She was a little afraid of this big, yellow-whiskered man, but Father went along, and soon the steam tractor operator was peering into Lydia's homemade cage. "That's a lark bunting, all right. Bobolinks are much lighter colored on the back than this bird. Lark buntings are great singers—every bit as musical as bobolinks, I think."

Lydia began hoping that Bobby, now named Bunny

129

since he was a bunting and not a bobolink, would sing for her. Bunny, however didn't sing. The only noise he made was an angry chirp whenever Greasy paid him too much attention.

◇◇◇◇◇

As spring wore on, Bunny seemed to thrive, and so did the crops. With thankful hearts, the farmers received timely rains, and the grain fields grew tall and green. Ben's sugar beets were doing well too.

In June the grain turned golden. One Saturday evening after a walk through the fields, Father announced, "By Monday we hope to start cutting the grain."

That Sunday afternoon, clouds with an eerie pinkish glow rolled up and blotted out the sun. Lightning flashed, and a clap of thunder followed. "We're going to have a storm," Lydia said, moving away from the window. She wished it were nighttime so she could pull the blankets over her head.

Outside on the porch, Stormy began whimpering loudly. Lydia asked, "May I let him in? He's afraid of thunder."

Mother looked at Father, who nodded. Just as Lydia opened the door, torrents of rain began to fall. Stormy slunk gratefully inside and lay down under the table. His body quivered.

Father stood at the window. "Hail!" he said suddenly. Then Lydia heard it, rattling on the roof.

"Those hailstones are the size of plums!" Joe shouted above the din.

In minutes the yard was white with ice, and still the hail came down, and the thunder crashed. Mother moved closer to Lydia. She understood how an eleven-year-old girl felt at such a time.

At last the noise subsided. Father said quietly, "The crops. They're smashed." His voice sounded hollow.

Lydia went to the window. The devastation was hard to grasp. Where there had been beautiful fields of waving, golden wheat, there was nothing but acres of flattened, shredded stalks.

"The Lord gave, and the Lord hath taken away; blessed be the name of the Lord," Father quoted from Job.

The kitchen was silent as the four of them continued staring out the window. The clouds had sped away, and already the sun was melting the drifts of hailstones.

"How do you think Ben's sugar beets look?" Joe asked finally.

"Pitiful, I'm afraid. Unless the hailstorm missed his place," Father replied.

"I guess we'll just have to pan for gold if we can't grow crops," Joe blurted out.

Father stared at him. So did Mother. Father said sharply, "We didn't come to Colorado to find gold."

Joe studied the toes of his boots. "But why not? What's wrong with gold?"

Father thought a while before replying. "The Bible says we are to make a living by the sweat of our brow. In other words—by working hard. I suppose panning for gold can be hard work too, but the Bible also says, 'Where your treasure is, there will your heart be also.'" He paused. "Faith in Jesus is the greatest treasure, Joe. If we seek for earthly treasure, I believe there's a danger that we don't leave enough room in our hearts for the greatest treasure of all."

Joe nodded. He gazed out across the glittering yard to the slashed wheat fields and thought to himself, *The power of God. Nothing else could have done this.* Suddenly Joe wanted a clear conscience before such an almighty God, and so he blurted out, "I-I've panned for gold."

"When?" asked Father quietly as though he wasn't really surprised.

"Last summer…and last fall. I quit in the winter. I knew you didn't approve."

"Do you understand now why I don't approve?" Father asked searchingly.

"Yes, I think I do. But I…I only wanted to help, you know…because the crops failed and all."

"We appreciate that you wanted to help," Father said softly. "And you do help. With your strong arms and willing heart." He smiled at Joe, and Joe smiled back.

That was the evening Lydia decided to set Bunny free.

"I'm pretty sure his wing is healed," she said as she carried the box out of the barn. Carefully she pried off the screen.

At first Bunny didn't understand what was happening. He had been in prison for so long that he hardly remembered his flying days. Then with a flutter of wings, he burst free and landed on the roof of the chicken coop.

There he stayed for a minute, flexing his wings as if to make sure they were all right. Then he soared high into the sunset sky, winging westward toward Pikes Peak.

"Come on, Bunny, sing!" Lydia shouted. "We want to hear a song from you. You never sang for us in the box."

It came floating down to Lydia and Joe—a series of crystal, trilling notes that went on and on as if the little songster could hardly stop!

"He's happy to be free," Lydia said breathlessly, tipping back her head to watch the tiny speck in the sky.

As for Joe, he thought he knew how that little bird felt.

19

The Hundred-Mile Trip

Sam and Polly's baby was born the week after the hailstorm. On the baby's first day, Father took Mother to see little Manasseh. On the second day, Father hitched up the team again to take Lisbet to be Polly's help for a few weeks. Much to Lydia's delight, she was allowed to go along.

As they turned onto the Peachys' lane, Lisbet exclaimed, "There comes Barbara with the children."

"She's just like me," Lydia said with a chuckle. "She can't wait to see her new nephew."

Abner and Noah were manfully tugging a little homemade wagon. On it sat one-year-old Hannah, chortling with glee as the wagon lurched over the rutted road.

All of them arrived at Polly's door together. From inside they heard Polly's voice calling, "Come in." She looked properly surprised to see so many family members at once. "We must be having a sisters' gathering today," she said.

Lydia went shyly over to the rocking chair where her sister sat with the baby. Manasseh looked like a doll, only better because he was real! His tiny red face was all scrunched up, and in a moment he let out a lusty cry. Lydia nearly jumped. To think that such a small baby could make so much noise!

Lisbet and Barbara took turns exclaiming over the baby and decided which grandpa he resembled. Then they all sat down for a visit while Barbara's three children played in the yard.

"On the way over here this morning, I felt almost like I was on the way to a funeral," Barbara confessed. "Those fields— They are such a sorry sight. To think that by now they would have been filled with rows of stocks…"

"It's a scene of disaster," agreed Polly. "Has Ben been talking about…about what he'll do to make money since his sugar beets aren't much good anymore?"

Barbara nodded. "In fact, he's made up his mind. He's starting off tomorrow for Ordway."

"The other Amish settlement in Colorado? What will he do there?" Polly asked.

"Haven't you heard? They're begging for seasonal workers over there. They have acres of melons, cantaloupes, and sugar beets ready to be harvested," replied Barbara.

"And they had no hail?" Lisbet asked.

Barbara shook her head. "No hailstorm there."

"Well, with our new baby and all, Sam won't be going

far away for work. He went to town today to see about getting work at the lumberyard."

"Jake is going to work for a carpenter," Lisbet told them.

"Will it be hard for you if Ben goes so far away?" Polly asked Barbara. "Ordway is a hundred miles away."

"In a way it's hard, yes, but I'll probably end up going too. If he finds a place for us to stay, he'll send for us, and I'll help pick melons," Barbara answered with a smile. "In this summer weather, even a tent would be good enough for us to live in."

"A tent!" cried Lisbet enviously. "I wish I could go too."

"Me too," echoed Lydia.

"Wait, Lisbet. I thought I'd hired you for my maid," Polly protested.

◇◇◇◇◇

In the end Joe got to go to Ordway. This is how it happened. Less than a week after Ben had left, Barbara drove to her in-laws' home. She was a fearless driver and had no problem hitching up two horses on her own.

After Father helped Barbara tie up the team, she went to the house with the three children. "I received a letter from Ben. He said that there's lots of work at Ordway, and he has a tent for us to live in. He even sent money for our train fare, but…we really can't afford to spend that money. I've decided I'd like to drive over there."

"With your horses?" Mother asked in surprise.

"I can't see why not. It would be good to have our horses over there. However, I was thinking that it would be very nice to have a strong young man along for the trip. It would take us a couple days, you know." Barbara locked eyes with fourteen-year-old Joe.

A grin lit Joe's face, and he instantly asked, "May I go, Father?"

"I guess you could pick melons too," Father said slowly.

"But what would you and Mother and Lydia do with me and Lisbet both gone?" Joe asked.

"I think we could manage. Don't you think so, Mother?"

Mother looked at Lydia. "You have been a good help in our garden. Maybe you can help Father with the chores too."

"Yes, I can," Lydia said stoutly. In a way she felt envious of Joe, but then again she was glad to stay home with Father and Mother.

On the very next morning, Barbara was back to pick up Joe and start off on their hundred-mile trip. "Why, she has a covered wagon!" exclaimed Lydia, staring out the window.

Mother came to have a look. "Isn't that something. She must have had a piece of canvas handy and used it to make a roof for their wagon. They'll be glad for shade from the sun on their long trip."

"It might rain too," Lydia pointed out.

"It might, but you know how seldom it rains."

Joe came downstairs with his parcel of belongings.

"Goodbye. Have a good summer," chorused Mother and Lydia as he went out the door.

"Goodbye!" he called back to them.

They watched as he climbed onto the seat beside his sister-in-law. As she handed the reins to him, three excited children bounced around in the back of the wagon among the pots and pans and bedding.

To Noah and Abner, riding in a covered wagon was fun—for the first three hours. After that Abner wondered if they were almost there. When his mother explained that it was going to take three days, he began to whimper. Noah complained that he was tired of sitting.

By noon, even Joe was glad for a break. Finding a grassy spot beside the road, he allowed the horses to graze. Barbara spread a cold lunch on a piece of oilcloth, and they all ate hungrily.

Noticing the children's drooping eyelids, Barbara said, "We'd better start off again before they fall asleep. They can take their naps in the wagon."

Joe found his own head nodding a few times as the horses plodded along. The scenery was monotonous. The flat prairie stretched for miles in every direction.

Barbara, Joe, and the three children
made the long trip to Ordway.

Suddenly Barbara said, "What's that up ahead? Looks like a town."

Joe jerked erect, realizing guiltily that he had been dozing. That was no way to drive a team! He focused on the cluster of buildings on the horizon. "Those houses don't look very good."

As they drew closer, they saw that all the buildings sagged in various stages of disrepair. Some roofs had caved in. The horses' hoofbeats sounded unnaturally loud as they clopped along between rows of forlorn, quiet buildings.

"I don't think anybody lives here," Joe remarked. "The whole place is dead."

"This must be a real ghost town," said Barbara.

Noah's head popped up suddenly behind them. "What's a ghost?"

"There's no such thing," his mother was quick to tell him. "Some people imagine they see ghosts, but there aren't any." Barbara gestured toward an old store with a crumbling false front. "Colorado has a lot of these ghost towns."

"They were built during the gold rush, I guess," said Joe.

"Yes, and when there was no more gold, the gold seekers quickly left town and moved on," responded his sister-in-law.

At the far edge of town, they passed the last old house with its rotten rafters and broken walls. "This is a picture of how it goes if we seek our happiness in the things of this world," mused Barbara. "We might think that a nice home or lots of money will make us happy, but those things are like a ghost town. They don't last. Lasting happiness comes from our faith in God."

Joe sat beside her and said nothing. Barbara had no idea what an impression her words made on him.

20

True Treasure

When the evening shadows lengthened, Joe asked his sister-in-law if they were going to stop at a farm for the night.

"That's what I was thinking," Barbara answered.

"I would be fine sleeping in someone's barn."

"Then let's turn in at this farm," Barbara suggested.

Joe drove the horses in the lane and pulled them to a halt in front of the barn. A man appeared in the doorway. Joe's heart sank when he saw the frown on his face.

Still, Barbara managed to ask, "Could we please sleep in your barn tonight? I'm from Wild Horse, and I'm on my way to Ordway to meet my husband. This is my brother-in-law."

With every word she said, the man's frown seemed to deepen. "We don't allow Gypsies on our place."

"Oh, I'm sorry. We'll leave," Barbara said hastily.

Joe bade the tired horses to start off again. He couldn't resist saying over his shoulder to the man, "We aren't Gypsies."

"Wait!" shouted a woman from the porch. Barbara and Joe turned to look in her direction and noticed her beautiful smile. "We have no spare bedroom, but you may sleep on our kitchen floor," she said.

Joe looked at Barbara. "Do I turn the horses around again?"

"Of course. We need shelter."

Joe directed the horses in a circle, through the grain stubble, and back onto the driveway. The man seemed friendlier now and helped him unhitch. "Guess I misjudged you," he said.

Joe answered, "That's all right. Maybe we do look like Gypsies. Can I help you with your chores?"

"If you want to work, you can feed the pigs. I'm Dan, by the way."

"And I'm Joe."

◇◇◇◇◇

So Joe and Barbara and the children spent the night, warm and dry and well fed. The next morning when they started off, the horses seemed refreshed. By nightfall, when they again found shelter with a friendly farm family, Barbara felt sure it would be their last night on the road.

On the third day, the scenery changed. Orchards lined the roads, and straight irrigation ditches ran between fields of cantaloupes, melons, and sugar beets. "We're almost there," Barbara told the tired children.

Noah scrambled to his feet and peered out from beneath the canvas. "Where's Daddy?"

"I'm not sure. We'll find him." Barbara scanned the dozens of workers bent over the rows of melons. There were many Amish men, but none looked familiar.

"We'll just keep on driving," Barbara told Joe. "If we don't find Ben soon, we'll stop and ask."

They passed field after field. The little boys kept asking where their daddy was, and their mother kept assuring them that they'd find him.

Suddenly a very surprised looking Ben appeared beside the wagon. "Well, what's this? Did you drive all the way from home?"

In one joyful bound, Noah catapulted out of the wagon and into his father's arms. Abner stayed on board but begged to be held. Hannah also stretched out her arms to Daddy. Ben ended up sitting on the tailgate with all three on his lap.

"Let me show you our tent," he said when the children allowed him to put them down. "Bring the horses over here please, Joe." He led them to a wide, grassy area where a number of tents were pitched. Numerous horses were staked out nearby.

Ben scratched his head. "I'm afraid there's no room in our tent for you, Joe. I didn't know you were coming, but I'm sure glad you did."

"I can sleep in the wagon," Joe offered.

Ben helped Barbara build a campfire to cook supper, just as many of the other workers were doing. By the time darkness fell, everyone was too tired to do anything other than roll into a blanket and fall asleep.

The next day, Joe started working in the fields with Ben. It was a new kind of work for him. Hour after hour he toiled with bent back, picking melons. Learning which ones were the ripest took a bit of practice. At first Joe couldn't pick nearly as fast as Ben could, but with each passing day, he grew quicker.

One morning Barbara said to Ben, "I need a few things at the store."

Ben looked at Joe, who sat on the grass finishing his breakfast. "Would you like to go to the general store in Ordway?"

"Sure," said Joe, always eager for something new. "Is there only one store?"

"Just the one general store called Merkel's. It's right on

the main street," Ben told him. "Here's some money and the list of things we need."

Walking down the town's dusty main street, Joe found the store easily. It had a tall false front and a blue-and-white sign that said Merkel's General Store.

Immediately inside the door was the wood paneled checkout counter. Behind it stood a middle-aged man with silver rimmed glasses and a bald head. "Hello," he said, smiling a welcome and stretching out his hand. "I don't believe I've met you before. I'm Tillman Merkel."

Joe shook his hand. "I'm Joe Yoder from Wild Horse. I'm working in the melon fields with my brother Ben."

"Ah. I know Ben. How can I help you?"

Joe showed him the list, and Mr. Merkel bustled off to get the items. Wandering down the aisle, Joe noticed another room at the back of the store. In it sat an old man with a purple blanket spread across his knees. He had a book and was reading aloud to himself.

As Joe passed by, the old man looked up. Suddenly his wrinkled face broke into a smile. "Why, if it isn't Joe Yoder!" he said with a voice that cracked.

Confused, Joe stopped in his tracks. *How does this stranger know me?* Then he recognized the old man. He was not a stranger at all. "Willie!" he said, going into the room.

"Didn't you know me at first?" the old prospector said with a chuckle. "I probably look older than I did the last time you saw me."

Joe recognized Willie.

"You were pretty sick the last time I saw you," Joe said. "Are you— Is your last name Merkel?"

"Yes, I'm Tillman's oldest brother. Had I never told you my last name?"

"I don't think so."

"What brings you way over here to Ordway?"

Joe told him about the hailstorm and the trip with

his sister-in-law. Willie listened quietly and then asked, "Could you do me a favor when you get back home?"

"I can try."

"My Bible is still there in my den. Tillman lent me his, but I'd enjoy having the one my mother gave me when I left home," Willie said.

Only then did Joe notice that the book on Willie's knees was a Bible. "I'll find yours for you, but it might be a while until I go home."

"That's all right." Willie's eyes took on a faraway look. "I only wish I'd read my Bible more in past years. That's what my mother asked me to do when she gave it to me, but I didn't listen."

Not sure what to say, Joe shifted his weight from one foot to the other.

"My mother didn't want me to go off hunting for gold," Willie explained, "but I was stubborn. I wanted to get rich quick. So Mother gave me a Bible, and in it she underlined this verse." Willie turned some pages in the Bible that rested on his knees. "Here it is, Matthew 13:44. 'Again, the kingdom of heaven is like unto treasure hid in a field; the which when a man hath found, he hideth, and for joy thereof goeth and selleth all that he hath, and buyeth that field.'"

Willie looked at Joe and said, "I didn't pay much heed to those words. I didn't understand them even though Mother had tried to tell me. 'Faith in Jesus, Willie. That's the greatest treasure of all. If we have Jesus, we don't need earthly treasure. We are willing to give it all up for His sake.'

"But like I said, I was a headstrong fellow. I went and did the opposite of what this verse in Matthew tries to tell me. I wasted my whole life in search of earthly treasure.

"Then when I was sick in the hospital, a minister came to visit me nearly every day. I asked him about this verse, and he said pretty much the same thing Mother had. Faith in Jesus is the true treasure. When He saves us from our sins by His blood, we are ready to give up earthly treasure."

Joe said, "That's what my parents say too."

Willie looked searchingly at the young man. "Do you remember how I once warned you not to let gold ruin your life?"

Joe nodded.

"And do you understand now why I said that to you?"

"I think I understand," replied Joe with a smile.

Other Great Harvest House Books by Rebecca Martin

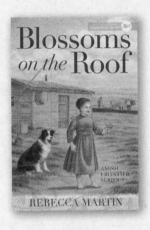

Blossoms on the Roof

The year 1894 brings hard times to the Yoders. When Father reads that free land is available in far-away North Dakota, the family packs up, says goodbye to family and friends, and boards the train for what they believe will be a better life out West. As soon as they step from the train onto the windswept prairie, however, they realize they have much to learn about homesteading.

They hurry to build their thatched-roof, sod house even as they plant a garden and till the fields. With each new experience—including the wildfire and long cold winter—they learn to trust God, embrace the pioneer spirit, and watch hardship turn into valuable life lessons.

Based on actual events from a time long ago, this unforgettable story from The Amish Frontier Series, perfect for ages 8 to 12, brings to life the Yoder family's move from a close-knit community to a pioneer life where they quickly discover how God is faithful to help in every situation.

About the Author

Rebecca Martin is a mother of four children, wife of Cleon, and author of numerous books. She and Cleon are members of the Old Order Mennonite church, semi-retired, and together they enjoy helping their married children. Rebecca also enjoys quilting as a pastime.

More Great Harvest House Fiction

The Pony Cart Adventure
by Elva Hurst

When eleven-year-old Elva finally finishes her chores on this beautiful summer morning, she hurries to the neighboring farm to see if her friend Linda can join her for an afternoon adventure. Come on along with the young Mennonite girls as they hitch up the pony, climb into the cart, and trot down the drive for a day filled with unexpected excitement.

This charming story, the first in the Farm Life Series, is based on author Elva Hurst's growing-up years on the family farm and written for children from seven to eleven years old. Reminiscent of days gone by, this simple tale is full of good-hearted fun.

Summer on the Farm
by Elva Hurst

Young Elva loves her summer days—once her daily milking, household, and gardening chores are done. In book two of the Farm Life Series, author Elva Hurst spins a simple tale of a summer spent splashing in the creek on hot afternoons and singing hymns with the other youth at the hymn sing. When news of a wedding surfaces, the neighboring Amish and Mennonite families all pitch in to make the day special for the young couple.

This delightful story is a beautiful picture of a young girl discovering joy in a simple life centered on a loving family, a tightly knit community, and an active faith in God... and just a little bit of mischief along the way.

Autumn Days
by Elva Hurst

This endearing story invites readers ages seven to eleven to share in a few of young Elva's adventures while working the autumn harvest with her family and attending school in rural Lancaster County. While abiding by the traditions of her Mennonite faith, she steps from one fun adventure to another.

Every family member, including children like Elva, help gather the fruits and vegetables from the orchards and gardens and then join the efforts to preserve the bounty. Is it all work and no fun? Certainly not! Find out what happens when Teacher invites the girls in Elva's class to a sleepover. Read about the day Elva decides to teach herself to play her brother's guitar—without his permission. Much can happen—and does—between chores!

When School Bells Call
by Elva Hurst

Readers ages seven to eleven will be drawn to this charming story that happened during a time not so long ago. Take a peek at life in a large, loving Mennonite family where everyone works together, faith is practiced daily, and fun happens often.

When the harvest starts in Lancaster County, it signals time for school to begin. Children help gather the fruits and vegetables from the gardens and prepare the one-room schoolhouse for the first day of school, and Elva loves it all!

One day Elva and her classmates plan a secret "food roll" to bless Teacher. They try their best to hide their giggles but erupt with laughter as Teacher shows her surprise. Then when her fifth-grade arithmetic lessons get Elva down, her brother suggests the perfect way to forget about her troubles—for a while anyway. And when the beautiful harvest moon is at its fullest, Elva steps quietly through the rustling corn fields to listen for…for what? What is it that makes Elva love autumn so much?